ELDERS OF ETHER

EMMA SHELFORD

ELDERS OF ETHER

Kinglet Books
Victoria BC, Canada

ISBN: 978-1989677353 (print)
ISBN: 978-1989677360 (ebook)

www.emmashelford.com

First edition: December 2021

CHAPTER I

Beaky eyed me with her beady little eyes. She let out a strident coo.

"I'm coming, greedy guts." I wrapped my sweater more firmly around my waist and rummaged in the bag I carried. Beaky cooed again, and I glared at her. "You're lucky I feed you at all, you little pest. It's only because you're an excellent watch-bird."

The pigeon strutted back and forth, looking proud. I rolled my eyes and scattered bits of old bread ends over the grass in front of my condo building. Beaky rushed forward and pounced on the morsels like they might jump away from her.

"I still don't know why you tolerate her," Caelus said with a long-suffering sigh. The elemental spirit that shared my body crossed his insubstantial arms. "Aren't I enough companion for you?"

"You're telling me you're jealous of a pigeon?" I dusted my hands and retreated to a nearby bench. "Don't worry, I have lots of room in my heart for two freeloaders."

Caelus snorted, but the purr of an expensive car engine pulling to the curb interrupted our conversation. I eyed the newcomers as they exited their sedan with slow yet graceful movements.

The driver stood straight and raised her face to the weak March sun that did its valiant best to dispel the threatening clouds surrounding it. She was a woman in her late sixties, her neck-length hair swept away from her face with warm highlights among the gray. Her intense eyes closed under carefully penciled eyebrows, and her strong jaw was only partially softened by age. Her leopard-patterned raincoat was practical with a nod to style that I hadn't expected from the rest of her demeanor. This was a woman who both prized form and function, ceremony and practicality.

Her companion adjusted her woolen peacoat and waited with barely concealed impatience for the driver to complete her sun salutation. She adjusted glasses on her nose and brushed her short gray hair off her forehead in an unconscious motion.

I tossed another few crumbs to Beaky and watched the pair from the corner of my eye. When they finally approached the condo, I tensed my muscles. I'd been in too many scrapes in the recent past to trust that random visitors to my condo building were always benign.

My instincts were correct. The pair left the front walkway and stopped in front of my bench. Beaky sidled away and glared at the two for interrupting her breakfast. She opened her beak with a strident coo, but they ignored her.

"Do I have the honor of addressing Morgan Feynman?" the driver said with a pleasant smile.

I narrowed my eyes at her. "Who are you?"

I half-rose from my seated position, and the woman sighed.

"I'll take that as a yes," she said.

Before I could stand fully, or open my mouth to speak, or do anything, the woman lifted her hand in a stopping gesture and spoke an illegible word. My world went black.

I awoke with a gasp. I wasn't groggy—far from it, my mind whirled with dizzying speed as I recalled my final moments before this one—and I sat up immediately.

"Now, now," a voice said in a firm yet kindly tone. "There's no need to overreact. The procedure won't take long."

My eyes glanced wildly around the space. It looked like a garden shed. A lawnmower was pushed against one wall, and a long counter held tools and bags of fertilizer. The door was propped open with a gas can so that light filtered through the

2

gap. I lay on a clean tarp on the cement floor, cold seeping through my jeans. I tried to move, but my hands and feet were unbearably heavy. Were they under the influence of an amulet? With my fingers out of commission, I had no way of manipulating threads save for my mouth, which was a difficult method unless another person was nearby.

The driver from before gazed at me with dispassionate eyes, her raincoat carefully folded over the handle of a lawnmower and the sleeves of her blousy silk shirt rolled up her arms. The other woman with glasses bustled around, lighting candles and incense. I coughed on the pungent smoke.

"Who are you?" I asked again. "Why did you kidnap me?"

"You didn't truly think you could get away with your antics at the Seed ceremony last month, did you?" The woman tsked as if correcting a disappointing child. "Walking around the city in broad daylight, not a care in the world. Let me introduce myself. My name is Hazel Jones, elder of the order you so foolishly embroiled yourself with." Hazel waved at the other woman. "This is Beatrice, another elder. We're here to exorcise your demon."

I choked with a mixture of laughter and disbelief. "My demon? I think you have the wrong person."

Hazel dismissed my objection with another wave of her hand. "Demon, spirit, whatever you like to call it. Forgive me, my terminology can be a little old-fashioned. The entity that gives you your powers. We will sunder it from your body, then you won't bother us anymore. It's high time I took a firmer hand in the situation. I clearly can't trust my underlings to do the job properly. I had high hopes for Thea Diamanto, but she is still young and inexperienced. We'll see. Perhaps by the time she's an elder, she will be ready, but not yet."

Hazel turned to examine Beatrice's work. I pulled at the ropes that bound my hands and feet and looked around the room, searching for anything that might help.

Caelus, I shouted in my head. *What are we going to do? Do you think they know what they're doing?*

Maybe, he said grimly, his presence filling my mind. *They're pretty powerful. Would I be sent back to the elemental plane? I'm not ready for that. We haven't collected nearly enough artifacts to satisfy my leader. And there's something about Hazel. Did you check out her threads?*

I stared at the older woman. Now that Caelus pointed it out, I noticed threads of seafoam green and bruise purple swirling around her body.

She's possessed too? I said in disbelief. *What element?*

Not an elemental, he corrected. *Not the right colors. No, I think she's a human possessing another human body. Just like you, but without me.*

I blinked, but we didn't have time to ponder the mysteries of Hazel. I resumed my frantic examination of the room.

Movement at the door caught my eye. A rust-colored pigeon strutted at the entrance, her neck bobbing and her black eye flickering over the interior.

Caelus, I said. *You transferred to Jerome at the orchard, remember?* Caelus had needed to stay behind to keep my friend Jerome from death's door while I'd fought the order for the Seed artifact.

I think Hazel has enough going on, he said.

Not Hazel. What if you jumped into Beaky? She's right at the door.

Caelus' feelings passed through my mind in a wave of scorn.

You want me to possess the flying rat-bird? You really don't think much of me, do you?

I'm open to suggestions, I said. *I wouldn't recommend an elder. Who knows how they could control you? But would Beaky even work?*

Before Caelus could respond, Hazel approached. Caelus retreated from my mind.

"It's time," Hazel said. "We're ready. I would say this

won't hurt a bit, but I have no idea. It might be terribly painful, for all I know."

"I'd work on your bedside manner," I muttered.

"Well, it's not as if I'm seeking your approval." Hazel took an old-fashioned key from a side table and held it up. Multicolored threads swirled around it, a sure sign the object was an amulet. What did it do? "One way or other, you will be rid of your spirit soon, then you can continue to live your short, meaningless existence in peace. You should be thanking me, really. Possession isn't a state most people strive to achieve."

Hazel held up her amulet, and I panicked. With a clucking noise, I called Beaky toward me in a signal that I'd been training her with. She waddled toward me eagerly, expecting a treat.

"Get the bird out of here," Hazel said irritably to Beatrice.

Caelus, I hissed in my mind. *Ready or not, you're going to Beaky.*

I rolled sideways and clucked at Beaky again. Before Beatrice could shoo the pigeon away, I concentrated with all my might on pushing Caelus' strands toward the nearby bird. He must have been helping, or at least not resisting, because his cluster of silver threads leaped from my stomach onto the bird. Beaky gave a surprised coo then burst into an explosion of flapping when Beatrice aimed a rake at her.

Emptiness reigned in my mind, and the threads of the world faded from my sight. The presence I'd grown used to having in my gut and mind was absent. The loss of Caelus was more shocking than I'd remembered, and I gasped.

Hazel mistook my gasp for one of fear at her antics. She smiled with her teeth, like a lioness about to pounce.

"Shall we begin?" Without waiting for an answer from me, she turned to the other elder. "Beatrice, the candle, if you please."

Beatrice handed Hazel a tall taper candle the color of fresh blood. Its flame flickered with the motion. Beatrice placed a wreath of leafless branches on Hazel's head, then touched her forehead with a thumb wetted from a glass of water on the table. Beatrice blew a puff of air into Hazel's face.

Hazel raised her hand with the key in her palm and stepped toward me. I wriggled away, but my magical constraints didn't let me go very far. Caelus was safe—I hoped—but I still didn't want Hazel performing strange exorcisms on my body without my permission. With little else to do, I spat at her. I was out of practice, and the spittle didn't reach her.

Hazel shook her head lightly. "Hold still, and we'll get this over with." With a motion like a striking snake, she jabbed the amulet at my stomach.

I screamed at the jabbing pain at the point of contact. Something was happening with the threads of the world, but I couldn't see them without Caelus. The blindness was unnerving, especially when zings of electricity shot through my body.

After that initial jab, the zings were far more manageable. Would they be if Caelus were still here? It was time to play along.

I screamed again and rolled my eyes back in my head. As the amulet threads crawled over my body, I shuddered and spasmed for dramatic effect. Beatrice glanced at Hazel with concern, but Hazel merely gazed at me in concentration, intent on her goal.

A full minute later, the painful tingling in my body subsided. I hunched over, trembling and wheezing—not entirely a sham—then glanced up at Hazel.

"Are you happy now?" I hissed. "My elemental is gone."

"Almost." Hazel placed her candle and key on the table and dusted her hands. "I only need two more things. I know you still have the artifacts. The order never recovered the Leaf after you stole it—a terrible breach of security that no one has yet remedied—and I know the Seed wasn't in the dirt as Thea imagined. I have ways of detecting artifacts, ways that the mothers and certainly the sisters do not have, and that patch of dirt held nothing but grass seed. Therefore, you must have secreted it away, and are now sitting on two of the most important objects in history."

I kept my face emotionless, but my heart sank. What method did she have of detecting artifacts? She wasn't possessed by an elemental, so she surely didn't have thread-vision. Maybe she owned an amulet that sniffed them out. My beaver keychain containing the Seed and Leaf burned a hole in my pocket, but I studiously kept my eyes on Hazel.

"Do your worst," I said to her. "You've already taken my elemental."

Hazel tsked again, and my stomach knotted at the sound. I detested condescension—my mind was nearly Hazel's age, even if my body wasn't—and I glared at the woman. She pulled out another key, this one an ornamental gold with a red jewel embedded in the bow. Unfazed by my eye-daggers, Hazel hovered the golden key over my body, sweeping across my torso like a metal detector over sand. She chanted under her breath as she did so. When she reached my pocket with the keychain, I held my breath. Would Hazel notice a change?

"Ah ha." Hazel's mouth twitched upward. "The key warms when an artifact is close, you see. Handy little device."

She placed the amulet on her table and reached into my pocket. I squirmed away from the unwelcome contact, but Hazel merely reached deeper until her fingers encountered metal. The smug satisfaction on her face was sickening.

"How eccentric," she murmured, examining the keychain with its besweatered beaver emblazoned on the front. "Though no one would think to look here, I'll give you that. Beatrice," she barked, and I jumped. "Give me the necklace."

Beatrice rummaged in a satchel on the ground and extracted a large golden locket.

"My keychain not special enough for you?" I said, although my heart squeezed in anguish at losing the artifacts. Caelus would be beside himself. He needed to collect enough artifacts so that the leader of his element, Air, wouldn't send him back to dormancy, which I gathered was a mindless purgatory for elementals. I strained at the magic holding my hands down to no avail.

"For these priceless artifacts?" Hazel huffed. "Hardly. You disrespect them by merely holding them, let alone keeping them trapped in this monstrosity. Shame on you."

"I don't live for your approval." I shook my head at her in disbelief.

Hazel plucked the artifacts out of the keychain's interior and carefully placed them inside the locket.

"All's well that ends well." She draped the necklace over her head and patted it on her chest. "You were an aggravation to my plans, but now more competent heads have prevailed, and you are defenseless and without our precious artifacts. You, in short, have no more part to play in this saga of hope and redemption. Enjoy your short, futile life, Morgan Feynman. I won't see you again."

Hazel swept out of the room. Beatrice scurried to pack away her candles and supplies in the satchel, then she approached me.

"You'll sleep this off soon," she said, then she pressed an amulet to my forehead. My last thought before succumbing to the darkness was, *not again.*

I blinked blearily awake when an insistent tapping drove into my skull. I was still in the same room, but Hazel and Beatrice were gone.

At the door, the source of the tapping revealed itself. Beaky rammed her beak against the metal wall of the shed with an incessant motion. Pigeons were good at bobbing their heads, after all. When she noticed my eyes open, she shuddered and ruffled all her feathers, then waddled close to me.

A second later, threads of the world bloomed before my eyes, and a familiar, comfortable presence filled my chest. Beaky left in an explosion of flapping, and Caelus' torso grew from my arm. His forehead was smooth with relief.

"You're finally awake," he said. "It's been ages. I was stuck in the rat-bird the whole time."

"What, Beaky isn't good company?" I sat and wiggled my toes. Beatrice must have removed the amulet's magic because my hands and feet were free to move.

Caelus sniffed. "Her mind is all over the place, just a rapid-fire succession of crumb-Morgan-wind-eggs-crumb-hawk-crumb. Terrible."

"But it worked." I stretched my arms over my head. How long had I been lying on that tarp? "You're still in the human world. We can still hunt for artifacts for your elemental mission."

At the mention of artifacts, my stomach dropped. Hazel had stolen the Leaf and Seed. We had nothing.

Caelus must have been watching the earlier exchange through the open door because his face fell almost comically at my reminder.

"What are we going to do?" he said, his voice as droopy as his face. He melted over my arm, his thread-body folded over and his head hanging. "I need those artifacts. They're our best lead. Why didn't we destroy them when we had the chance?"

"We thought they might help us retrieve the Thorn," I said. "It was a gamble, and we lost. But just because Hazel took them doesn't mean we can't get them back. And now we have an advantage."

"We have nothing."

"We," I said louder than Caelus' objection. "Have each other, which is more than Hazel thinks we have. She assumes I am powerless. That's our trump card. We'll keep it secret until an opportune moment. It gives us breathing room to work, because no one will be hunting me to search for artifacts."

"Because we don't have any," Caelus muttered, but he floated to an upright position again.

"So, we'll change that." I sat up straight. "Hazel has two of the three artifacts. She'll be searching for the Thorn with renewed zeal. We need to get it before her."

I jumped up from the tarp, filled with renewed vigor. Hazel's antics, instead of forcing me into submission as she'd intended, had done the opposite. Fire filled my belly. We had a mission, and Hazel was an obstacle. I knew how to deal with obstacles. Hazel might have the artifacts, but I would make her work hard to keep them.

"How do we get the Thorn before Hazel?" Caelus swayed at my motion. His mouth twisted with his fearful hope. "That clue you found wasn't as clear as you thought earlier. We visited that cave under the hightide mark, the one you thought the Book of Souls was talking about, but it didn't have the Thorn."

"But we're not alone." I straightened my jacket and strode to the door. It was unlocked, and I swung it open with gusto. Outside, a manicured lawn led to the back side of my condo building. "There are order members on our side. Too many secrets in the order have turned some sisters against them. And who better to help us uncover the truth of the Thorn's location than those versed in its lore since birth?"

CHAPTER II

I walked into the coffeeshop Sacred Grounds late the next day after a tension-filled walk. I hadn't left my condo since returning from the exorcism. Every person I passed on the sidewalk was a possible order member, and it was with relief that I flung open the coffeeshop door.

It was a slow time at the shop, and only Amanda worked behind the counter. Miranda had suggested the locale for our clandestine meeting. It was natural that we would meet here—the sisters and I often did, after all—but with loyal Denise on her day off, we could speak freely. Amanda would join us when she could get away from customers.

"Tea, please," I told Amanda. "Large."

She nodded and winked a pale blue eye at me, and I bit my lip to prevent a smile. It was a good thing Denise wasn't here because Amanda was terrible at staying clandestine.

"It's pretty slow today," she said, her ginger ponytail swinging as she prepared my tea. "I should be able to join you."

I nodded and retreated to a table in the corner to wait for Miranda. When the slender, dark-haired girl finally entered the coffeeshop, my heart quickened. Joy was with her, her blond curls as perfectly formed as ever. Joy and Miranda worked down the road at Cut Right, a hair salon run by order members.

I took a sip of tea to hide my confusion. At the Seed ceremony last month when I'd stolen the artifact from the order, Joy hadn't stopped me, but neither had she helped. A bandage still covered her temple where an order member's errant shovel swing had knocked her unconscious.

Miranda must think Joy was trustworthy. My gut agreed—Joy was the last person I'd consider duplicitous, and I thought of her a friend—but my mind was suspicious. I hoped Miranda was right.

The two waved at me then ordered drinks after a whispered conversation with Amanda. When they approached the table, beverages in hand, I was composed and ready for them.

"What happened?" Miranda said after sliding into her seat and leaning forward. "You didn't give any details on the phone."

I glanced at Joy, who was taking off her coat and arranging it on the back of her chair. Miranda correctly interpreted my glance.

"Joy's with us," she said quietly. Joy looked sharply at me and nodded with earnest vigor. Miranda shot a swift look around, but no one sat near us. "She's as disillusioned with the order as I am. The mothers and elders can't be trusted with the artifacts, not after they've lied to us for so long."

"It's despicable," Joy whispered in her rich voice. "Our whole lives, we've been kept in the dark and fed B.S. It's time that stopped."

I nodded. It was time to place my trust in these women. That was a hard step for me, but it was the only way I could move forward with my goals. Caelus needed me to take some risks for the rewards he desperately sought.

"The elders Hazel and Beatrice kidnapped me yesterday," I said. The others gasped with their eyes wide. Miranda gripped the table with white knuckles. "It's beginning to be quite a habit with the order. Hazel performed a ritual to—" I paused. I'd never told them about Caelus and the source of my wind powers. Was I ready to do that today?

Caelus' approval hummed through my torso. He must be desperate if he wanted to reveal our secret to the others. He needed those artifacts back, and soon.

"To exorcise the elemental spirit that possesses me and gives me my powers," I finished.

Joy choked. "You're possessed?" she hissed.

"What does that even mean?" Miranda said, her grip on the table unyielding.

"Do you have powers anymore?" Amanda said. She'd clearly heard the last part of my announcement. She flopped onto the remaining chair and joined her sisters in a wide-eyed stare at me.

"Hazel has powerful amulets," I conceded. "But my elemental and I are clever. His name is Caelus, by the way. No, she didn't manage to sunder us, but she believes she did."

"Damn it." Joy thumped the table with her fist. A patron on the far side of the room looked up with surprise. "How could she do something like that? I didn't even know it was possible. Hell, I didn't even know someone could be possessed by an elemental spirit. Hazel clearly knew that and how to get rid of one."

"What else do the elders know that we haven't been told?" Miranda's lips tightened. "It's unacceptable. Are we a part of the order or not? Who do they think will be elders one day? Don't we deserve a bit of trust after everything we've done for the order?"

"They're grooming you," I said. "It's not unprecedented. The ones who show the most potential and willingness to follow the order's values will be gradually shown more and more. If they prove themselves, eventually all will be revealed. But they aren't going to let just anyone join the inner circle."

"You see this so much more clearly than we do." Miranda put her head in her hands. "I feel so stupid. How could I not have noticed all this before?"

I put a comforting hand on Miranda's shoulder. "It's easy to see from a distance," I said gently. "But it's how you were raised. That's a difficult position to gain perspective from."

I took a sip of my cooling tea while the others stewed in their anger and disillusionment.

"This can't go on," Joy said suddenly. "They have to be stopped. If half of what we know is true—the power infusion to the mothers and elders, their lack of care about the promised utopia—then we're in trouble when they find the Thorn."

"In more trouble than before, definitely," I agreed. "Hazel also stole the Leaf and Seed from me."

Three pairs of eyes stared at me.

"You had the artifacts?" Amanda said faintly. "I thought the Seed was lost."

"Powers, remember?" I waved my hand at her. "I can see things more clearly than most. It wasn't difficult to retrieve the Seed from that pile of dirt, and I've had the Leaf since that fiasco with your sister Starr. I thought I had a lead on the Thorn—the mothers' copy of the Book of Souls mentioned a cave hidden underwater—but I checked out my idea and came up empty handed."

"What do you want, Morgan?" Joy said, her voice without its usual warmth.

I sat back and crossed my arms. "I want to destroy all three artifacts. They are dangerous—giving untold powers to unscrupulous people is not my idea of sensible—and, as elemental magic in the human world, they don't belong here. My elemental spirit, Caelus, that's his mission on Earth, to find and destroy all the artifacts we can lay our hands on." I tilted my head. "Does that bother you? Speak now if we're not on the same page."

All three were silent for a long while. Amanda's expressive face worked with emotion, and Miranda covered her mouth with her hand. Joy's eyes were closed, and she took deep, steady breaths.

"It's hard to let go of the promised utopia," Amanda said finally.

"But it was a sham from the start," Miranda blurted out. "They lied about everything else. How do we know the utopia was real or just a pretty story to make us follow along?"

"Maybe it's better this way," Joy said. "Could humans handle connection to everything? I don't know what that would even be like."

A long pause allowed the three to digest their new reality.

Joy eventually shook her head, and her curls bounced.

"I don't know about destroying the artifacts," she said. "But we need to get them out of the hands of the Elders, for sure. I'll help however I can."

The other two murmured their agreement, and I nodded back. My chest warmed at their acceptance. It was good to feel part of a group, even if that group was destined for mayhem and destruction. A thought crossed my mind.

"How many people are in the order?" I said. "We need solid numbers to know what we're facing. There are nine sisters, and five mothers."

"There are only three elders," Amanda said, counting on her fingers. "Agatha—you saw her at the Seed ceremony—she's the leader, although Hazel really runs the show. There's Beatrice, too. That's it."

"Anyone else connected—family members not being trained for sisterhood, for example—don't know anything about the order and its business," Joy said. She swirled her coffee with an absentminded motion.

"What about allies?" I asked. "Is it just you three? What about former sisters and mothers who didn't make the cut? Is everyone else still walking the party line?"

Amanda shook her head. "People who leave the order tend to 'forget' everything about it, or at least think that it was a dream or a game they played. Convincing them that it was all real is a waste of time—trust me, I've tried before."

"Rosemary's not in the order anymore, but she knows plenty," Joy said. "But's she's—not really herself these days. Not since Thea took over her mind at the Seed ceremony. I guess we can include her for now. She's very eager, but—well, you'd have to see her to understand. I assume the order will make her 'forget' soon too, but Hazel has been away a lot lately, and I think she's the one who takes care of that."

"Denise and Wanda are one hundred percent with the order." Miranda's brow furrowed. "Sarah is too young to know anything—she only just joined, so she's with them—and I don't know about Jasmine. I'll have to tread carefully around Shu, feel out where she stands on this."

"The mothers are all pro-order," Amanda said. "I'd be surprised if any of them turned. Same with the elders, although Agatha isn't a threat anymore."

"I can't believe Agatha is power-hungry like that." Joy shook her head. "She's always so passionate about the utopia. Do you think she's been hoodwinked, too?"

"I don't know, but we need answers." Miranda opened her mouth to say more, then she snapped it shut with a clack of her teeth. She grinned brightly across the room and raised her voice. "Denise, hi! Want to join us for a drink?"

I glanced at Joy, who looked shocked but swiftly hid her expression. When Denise walked behind the counter to fix herself a drink, Miranda hissed to us.

"We'll meet again soon, somewhere more private. Got it?"

I was dying to continue our meeting, but discretion was key. The order needed to see that I was powerless and no threat to them. Coffee with other order members wasn't suspicious— we were friends, after all—as long as no one loyal to the order suspected our topic of discussion.

Besides, I had other concerns. Tonight, Jerome and I were going on a date.

I walked swiftly home, my eyes peeled for suspicious walkers. I ignored the spring wind that still managed to bite through my coat and weasel its cold fingers down my collar. My stomach flopped with long-forgotten butterflies. Why was I nervous? Just because we'd thrown around the word "date" didn't mean that it wasn't just a get-together with Jerome. He was the same person, and I was the same experienced woman I'd always been. My betraying stomach flopped again, and I

16

sighed. My body was still young and prone to nerves. That must have been it.

A small voice whispered that my mind and body were intimately connected at this point, but I dismissed it by the time I entered my condo. Instead, I pondered the contents of my closet. It was just Jerome, who had seen me at both ends of my wardrobe spectrum, but I still needed to set the right tone. Too casual meant I didn't respect him and this date. Too formal and he would wonder if we were going to talk business. Too revealing might lead us down roads more quickly than I was prepared for.

In the end, I went with a fitted blouse and tight jeans. Outside my condo, Jerome stood on the sidewalk, waiting for me. My chest tightened with a pleasurable ache, and I strode down the walkway toward him.

He turned, and his face transformed with his smile. I returned the expression and slid my hand into his without thought. He looked down at our clasped fingers in surprise, but I didn't want to overthink it. His warm hand, large over my slight one, felt right. I squeezed it and pulled him down the sidewalk.

"Where are we going?" I asked. "You wanted to surprise me."

"Where would we be going if you were choosing?"

I tilted my head in thought. Jerome's hand in mine was distracting, as was his arm brushing mine on occasion, but I answered as well as I could.

"Old me would have chosen Chez Michel." I grinned when Jerome's hand twitched in mine at the mention of an expensive local restaurant. I squeezed it again reassuringly. "New me, however, would far prefer the taco place on Cormorant Drive."

Jerome's shoulders relaxed. "Good," he said gruffly. "Because I wanted to take you to a pizza joint just past the Skytrain terminal. It's tiny, but their crust is superb."

"If a baker is saying that, then I need to try it."

The pizza place was a small as Jerome had warned, but when he opened the inset red door in a brick and windowed frontage, the scent of warm tomato sauce and melted cheese permeated the room with delectable aromas. I breathed deeply as Jerome led me to a seat by the window under a raftered ceiling. The table was lit by a hanging lamp that glowed red through an old-fashioned stained-glass lampshade.

"What will you have?" Jerome said over his menu once we were seated and the server had brought us drinks. He wore his usual buttoned-up polo shirt, and a wave of desire washed over me when I imagined what must be underneath.

I pushed the menu toward him, too distracted to choose. "You order. I trust you."

Jerome's mouth quirked, and when the server came to our table, he ordered two pizzas with confidence.

"What's new with you?" Jerome said. "It feels like it's been a while."

"It does." I looked at him over my glass of red wine. Should I tell him about my latest kidnapping? Last time I'd been snatched, I'd almost had to wrestle him back into his chair to prevent him racing after the culprits and dealing out justice.

But if I were dating Jerome, didn't he deserve the truth? I suppressed a chuckle of mirth. I had many layers of truth. How far did I want to pull the cover off my life?

But Jerome had been part of this whole order fiasco from the start. He deserved to know.

"I was kidnapped again yesterday," I said in a calm tone.

Jerome choked on his wine. "What?" he said in a strangled voice. "Who? What happened? Are you okay?"

"I'm fine." I waved his concern away. "And by the order, who else?"

"This can't keep happening." Jerome's face was dark, and he could barely get words out through his tight jaw. "Tell me who it was, and I'll make sure it doesn't happen again."

I considered him. A battle raged beneath Jerome's usual

calm exterior. Something darker, tougher lurked underneath.

If I were being honest with myself, it intrigued me. I had my own hidden depths, after all. I was no saint—a particularly shameful lapse in judgement as my former self March Feynman had almost ended in a woman's murder—and it somehow relieved me to find Jerome might have his own dark secrets.

Another part of me, possibly fueled by my youthful body, thrilled at the thought of Jerome wanting to hunt someone down to protect me. I didn't need protection, but a primal part of me enjoyed his offer.

But I didn't want him hurt. Hazel was equipped with powerful amulets, and if Jerome confronted her, it would almost certainly end badly. I reached out and touched his hand lightly.

"Thank you for the offer, but I don't think it's wise to antagonize them. They have magical weapons. Besides, they now think I'm not a threat, so they shouldn't bother me anymore."

Jerome sat back with a disgruntled look. "If you're sure. Because I don't mind at all. I'm good at getting my point across." He shook his head, discomfort written across his face as if he'd said too much. "What did they want, anyway?"

"They wanted to exorcise Caelus from me, as well as steal the artifacts."

"Did they succeed?" A flash of hope flickered in Jerome's eyes, quickly followed by guilt.

He hadn't come to terms with Caelus in my body yet. I couldn't blame him—it was a bizarre situation at the best of times—but I was pleased to see the guilt that followed. Losing Caelus would mean no more powers, which I wasn't ready to accept. I knew I could handle myself without Caelus—the Seed ceremony had proved that—but I could still achieve far more with his help.

Caelus blossomed out of my arm, invisible to everyone

except me.

"I'm still here, lover boy," he said.

Jerome jumped, and his face drained of color. "Don't scare me like that," he gasped. "And keep your voice down."

"No one else can hear me except you two," Caelus said. "I have control enough for that little trick. Don't worry about me. We've been doing this for a while, now."

"This is so weird," Jerome muttered. "I forgot this was dinner for three."

"Caelus, get back in there," I hissed. "Honestly."

Caelus grumbled but melted back into my arm and retreated to a silver ball of threads at my stomach. Jerome gripped his wineglass. I rested my fingers on his wrist.

"You're going to break it," I said softly.

Jerome put the glass down and sighed. "I'm sorry. Caelus is really hard to get used to."

"I know. You have nothing to apologize for. He's a handful." I paused. "I'm a handful."

Jerome leaned across the table. "You're worth it," he said with intensity, and my heart pounded. Our faces were close, but not close enough for my liking. I leaned in.

A ping from Jerome's phone broke the moment. I sat back, trying to control my body's reaction. Jerome looked at his phone and read the message. His expression darkened.

I shivered. It was astonishing how his face could be soft and open in one moment, and terrifyingly hard the next.

He shoved the phone back into his pocket with more force than necessary and took a deep breath.

"Is everything okay?" I asked.

"Yeah." Jerome's assurance didn't show on his face. "Give me a moment, will you?"

Without waiting for a reply, he leaped out of his seat and strode to the exit. I watched, open-mouthed, as he pushed the door open and rushed outside and out of view.

CHAPTER III

My hand swirled my wineglass for lack of something better to do. What had riled Jerome up to the point of fleeing outside? What news could have possibly provoked such a reaction? A death in the family, maybe, or news of illness. Would he tell me what was wrong?

By the time Jerome returned, the pizza had arrived, as well as his relaxed demeanor. Whatever had bothered him was now either dealt with or buried deep enough to avoid detection.

I took my cue from Jerome, although I was dying to know what he was hiding from me. But if I wanted his secrets, I had to be prepared to share mine. Was Jerome ready to hear that this wasn't my first body? I wasn't sure.

The rest of dinner passed in agreeable conversation, and it was with a full stomach and contented mind that I exited the restaurant hand in hand with Jerome. He was quieter on the walk back to my condo, as if the effort of maintaining a happy façade had drained him.

I wasn't someone who minded a little silence, and I allowed him to dwell on whatever had upset him earlier. Content radiated through me at his hand in mine.

Too soon, we reached my condo door. My mouth almost opened to invite him up to extend our evening, but I hesitated. Was I ready for where that might lead?

Jerome focused on my face, finally seeing it after the last few minutes of absenteeism.

"I'm sorry," he said quietly. "I was distracted."

"You know you can tell me anything, right?" I put my palm on his cheek, and he leaned into it. "I'm here for you."

He sighed, and his eyes dropped to my lips. We were close, now, and my hand's connection drew our heads closer together. My breath hitched, and my eyes closed without intent.

Our lips met, and in that instant, my entire body relaxed into his. The space between us vanished as if it had never been, and all I could feel was the radiant heat of his hard body pressed against mine. My hands ran up his well-muscled arms and twined around his neck, while those same arms wrapped around my waist and held me tight against him.

When I took a breath, gasping a little from the intensity of our kiss, Jerome's arms stiffened, and he pulled away.

"Caelus," he said. "Is he still here?"

"Always," Caelus said, emerging from my arm. "I thought you understood that by now."

Jerome shivered and disentangled himself from my grasp. I glared at Caelus.

"Really?" I said. "Why are you out here?"

"I thought it was rude to not acknowledge Jerome's question."

I sighed heavily through my nose. My body screamed to get closer to Jerome again, but the uncomfortable look on his face told me that option was over for tonight. He chuckled awkwardly.

"Sorry," he said. "I'm still getting used to him."

"I know." I looked up at the sky, trying to gain control of myself. "I'll figure something out. Soon."

It took a long shower and a longer cup of tea to calm myself enough for sleep. My alarm awoke me early the next morning, and I rose without hesitation. If our renegade group were to meet in secret, some sacrifices had to be made. Sleep was the sad but necessary cost to ensure we could meet undetected before the others went to work or university.

I traced the familiar path to Rosemary's house and knocked on her red door. Barely a few seconds ticked by before it opened with a rush of air.

"Come in, come in," Rosemary hissed at me. "Make sure you weren't noticed."

I blinked at Rosemary's paranoia but stepped smartly into her tiny hallway that spilled into the living room. Miranda, Joy, and Amanda were already seated there, perched on armrests and rubbing tired eyes. Rosemary clapped her hands, and the others jumped.

"Good, you're all here," she said. "Are we all ready to take the order down?"

Rosemary was stepping into a leadership position by default, as the former head sister, and the others looked content to allow her. I, however, had no intention of receiving orders from Rosemary. At best, she was incompetent. At worst, volatile. Clearer heads should take control of matters here.

"Yes, thank you all for coming," I said smoothly. Rosemary looked at me oddly, but I smiled at her and continued talking. "These are strange times indeed, when you must turn against everything you've been brought up to believe. I understand how hard that must be." The others nodded and glanced at each other in relief that I had acknowledged their pain. "But for the sake of the world, we must stop the order from completing their mission. We are the only ones who can."

"But how?" Amanda said with a helpless shrug. "The mothers and elders have powerful amulets, and we can't even get a hair straightener ring from Filippa. She's got a tight grip on all the sisters' amulets."

The others nodded somberly. I twisted my mouth in thought.

"We need to brainstorm our strategy." I turned to Rosemary. "Do you have paper and a pen?"

Rosemary, who had brightened at my notice, wilted and scurried to fulfill my request. She returned and poised herself to write. I allowed her this concession. It was easier to chair a meeting if one didn't have note-taking duties to attend to.

"What are our goals?" I asked the room at large. "What do

we want to achieve?"

"Stop the order from completing the mission," Miranda piped up.

"Yes," I said. "But what would make them stop?"

"Lock them all up with a taste of their own amulets," Rosemary muttered.

"That's certainly an option," I said in a neutral tone. "But maybe there are others. Anyone? What do they need to complete their mission?"

"We have to steal the artifacts back from them," Joy said loudly, her eyes narrowing with intent.

"Yes," I said. "And, I posit, find the Thorn before they do."

"That's impossible," Miranda said, defeated. "We have no clue where the Thorn would be. The elders are the ones in charge of looking for it. They have the full Book of Souls. Who knows what clues are in there?"

"I agree, having the Book of Souls would increase our chances of finding it," I said. "But, you forget, we have a secret weapon. My elemental spirit might be of use in deciphering any clues in the Book."

Rosemary's eyes gleamed. "We need to steal the Book of Souls," she said. "But the full copy this time. Oh, I'm dying to see what it says. What have they been hiding from us?"

"Good." I clapped my hands. "We are agreed, we need the Book of Souls. I also think it couldn't hurt to have a few more order members on our side. What's the status with Shu? Do you think she might be swayed? I don't want anyone who will rat us out."

"She might." Miranda played with the tassels of a cushion on her lap. "I don't know."

"Why don't you feel her out," I said to Miranda. "You work with Shu in the salon. Catch her on her own sometime and casually mention your doubts, see how she responds. Keep leading her further down the path of revealing her true feelings until you're sure."

"I can do it," Rosemary blurted out. "I can find out what she's thinking."

I glanced at Joy, who gave me an expressive eyebrow. Maybe Joy was right, and Rosemary would be more trouble than she was worth. I couldn't imagine her approaching anything with the stealth and subtlety this mission required.

"I'm sure you could," I said smoothly. "But why don't we give Miranda a chance first? I don't want to scare Shu off and make her run back to the order if too many people approach her at once."

"I don't know." Miranda looked troubled. "Do you think it will work? She won't catch on to what I'm trying to do?"

"You'll do well," I assured her. "Just don't mention any names until you're convinced of her sincerity. Now, we need more information on the Thorn and where the elders keep a copy of the complete Book of Souls. Joy, why don't you chat up the elders for information?"

Joy's eyes popped wide. "Me?" she said. "Are you sure?"

"You're an excellent conversationalist." What I meant was that she could chat the ear off a rabbit, but I needed to butter up her confidence. "Find a way to slip in some questions among innocent comments. I have full faith in you."

Joy gulped but nodded. Both she and Miranda looked nervous, but all the sisters seemed relieved that I'd taken the reins of this mission. My shoulders relaxed at the familiar sensation of leadership. It was a natural position for me since I'd occupied it for many years before switching into this body. I knew how to handle people.

The others left one by one, with various expressions of nervousness and excitement on their faces. I was about to follow Joy when Rosemary's hand on my arm stopped me.

"Morgan," she said, her eyes filled with a light of fervor

that immediately put me on my guard. "This isn't enough. We need to do more."

Joy edged back into the house and exchanged a glance with me.

"This is a good plan," Joy said carefully. "We need to be cautious."

"Cautious?" Rosemary's eyes widened past surprise into madness. "There's no time for that. The order needs to pay. Hazel could find the Thorn at any moment, then she and the other mothers and elders would have all the power. They would rule us! Can't you see that the situation is dire? Am I the only one who sees clearly?"

Rosemary turned away from us to pace the room. Caelus emerged from my arm and spoke to me alone.

"Maybe she's more trouble than she's worth," he said.

"Do you think Thea's messing with her mind did permanent damage?" I asked him and Joy quietly.

"Maybe." Joy watched her former sister with worry. "She's not acting normally."

"I agree," I said. "This is beyond passion for vengeance. I don't know if we can trust her."

"Calm her down with threads," Caelus suggested. "Then spin her a line about your plans for long in the future."

"I have this," I murmured to Joy. To Rosemary, I said, "You seem tense, Rosemary. Sit with me on the couch for a moment."

Rosemary looked too amped up to sit, but after a moment's hesitation, she flopped onto the couch. I didn't waste time and sat beside her with my fingers at the ready.

"Close your eyes," I instructed. "Take a deep breath. We'll figure this out. Calm heads must prevail."

Rosemary leaned her head back and closed her eyes. Her breathing was ragged, but she tried to even it out.

My fingers reached to her head and flew around her temples. Caelus retreated into our body and nudged my hands in the right direction. Before long, Rosemary's breathing was even without being forced, and a faint smile crossed her lips.

"I do feel better," she said without opening her eyes. "Good idea, Morgan."

"I'm glad," I said in a steady tone. "Now, for the plans. We will certainly pursue the full Book of Souls, but this is a delicate operation. It will take a few weeks to plan. We'll let you know when we're ready for you, okay? Hazel hasn't yet found the Thorn, and she's been looking for decades. We have time."

"We have time," Rosemary repeated. She turned on her side and drew her legs into her chest. "We have time."

Joy disappeared and returned with a blanket from Rosemary's bedroom. She draped it over the sleepy woman. I stood up carefully from the couch, and we retreated outside.

"Will it keep her calm and out of our way?" Joy asked me.

"It should do." I zipped up my coat and took a deep breath. "We can't afford to have her barge in and ruin everything. This is for the best."

We parted ways after that. Joy headed to her job at the salon Cut Right, and I walked directly to the Lebanese grocery store on Cormorant Drive. I wanted to check in with Amir, the proprietor, and see whether he had implemented any of my business suggestions. My future entrepreneurial venture hinged on his testimonial.

"Morgan!" Amir cried out when I entered the grocery which was heavily scented with briny olives and fresh flatbread. "Wonderful Morgan. Come, choose your favorite cheese. On the house."

I blinked. Amir was always friendly, but this greeting was excessive, even for him. What had prompted it?

"Thank you, Amir." I walked closer to his station behind the cheese counter to avoid shouting past the few customers shopping at this early hour. "How is business?"

"Booming, thanks to you." He dug into a salty sheep's feta

I liked and cut away a generous slab. "I've followed your plan to the letter, and already, our profits are up twenty percent. Now, maybe it is fluke, maybe not, but my heart tells me it is real, and it's due to your changes. I don't know how to thank you."

"Well," I said cautiously. "A good testimonial wouldn't go amiss."

Amir flapped his hand at me and slid the feta into a plastic tub.

"I have already told all my friends about your help. They want to hire you." He dug into the pocket of his apron and held out a folded sheet of paper. "Here, the names and their businesses. They will pay for your services, no problem. They are only angry at me for getting you first."

He chuckled richly and handed over my cheese. I took it and the paper with disbelief.

"Really?" A smile cracked open my face with genuine happiness. Maybe this venture would take off, after all. And none too soon, according to my almost exhausted bank account.

"Of course!" Amir beamed at me. "Call them right away. And come back every week for your cheese, on the house."

I thanked Amir again and picked up some dates—my manners couldn't allow me to walk out without purchasing something—then walked out of the grocery, light on my feet. As soon as I left the building, my phone was plastered to my face.

"Mr. Lomidze? Hello. My name is Morgan Feynman. Amir Khoury might have mentioned me…"

I leaned against the park bench with a happy sigh. Amir must have shared praise so glowing his friends had needed sunglasses, because I now had three new businesses to analyze and improve, all with paychecks attached. Finally, my life was taking shape, away from my past as March and out of the turmoil of becoming Morgan. I was landing on my feet, and I loved it.

If only a certain order would stop trying to end the world.

I tweaked the air around me to blow puffs of warm wind on my face to counteract the early spring chill. Caelus slithered up from my arm, the corners of his mouth turned downward.

"What's up with you?" I asked. "Are my happy vibes not reaching your threads?"

"It's the artifacts." Caelus gave a heartfelt sigh. "We lost two of them. We've only destroyed two others so far, and the Leaf and Seed were supposed to count in our tally. Now they're gone."

"We have the sisters on our side," I reminded him. "We're not alone in this. I have them on assignments."

"But will they find anything? I don't know. It all feels so hopeless. I almost wonder…" Caelus trailed off, and I looked at him closely.

"Wonder what?"

"Oh, nothing. Forget I said anything."

"Spill it," I said. "Don't make me dig around in your mind. It's chaotic in there."

Caelus frowned at me with the ghost of his usual zest.

"I wondered if I should ask for help from the elemental plane." He pulled a thread from his hand and fidgeted with it. Small puffs of breeze wafted past my face with the motion.

"Is that an option?" I said in surprise. "Of course you should. Any help we can get is welcome."

"It's not that simple. I'll have to admit that I lost two artifacts. They'll wonder why I didn't destroy them immediately, then they'll question whether I'm the right elemental for the job. Losing the Leaf and Seed is a sign of failure, and I can't afford to fail."

"It's risky, is what you're saying." I drummed my fingers

on my thigh. An older gentleman shuffled past, and I waited until he was out of earshot before continuing our conversation. "We might get answers, or you might get sent back to dormancy."

Caelus shuddered, his disgust for that option clear. From what he had described to me, I didn't wish dormancy for him.

"I'm not saying we shouldn't pursue that option," I said after a moment. I wasn't ready to lose Caelus yet, either for my own sake or for his. "But maybe we should try a few other things first. Save it for later."

Caelus nodded fervently. "Good idea."

CHAPTER IV

After my business triumphs, I deserved a treat. Caelus melted into my arm, and I headed for Upper Crust, the bakery where Jerome worked. The day was sunny and crisp, although a breeze with a hint of warmth ruffled my hair with the promise of spring.

The server at the till greeted me with a friendly smile and prepared a plate of three lemon tarts without me saying a word.

I laughed. "Thanks, Kaylee. I guess I'm predictable. What would you say if I asked for a scone instead?"

"I'd ask if you were feeling okay," she said with a grin.

I chuckled and paid for my tarts and coffee, then found a seat against the wall. Jerome was working in the back, ladling batter into muffin tins. After he slid the tins into the industrial oven where loaves of bread already resided, their crusts turning from pale to a delicious golden brown, he slipped off his apron and walked over to join me.

"Morning, stranger," I said, then I frowned. "What happened to you?"

Jerome sat with a grunt of discomfort. His lip was split with a raw-looking wound, his right cheekbone sported a nasty bruise, and he favored his left arm.

"It's nothing," he said gruffly. "I'm fine."

"You are not fine. You were beat up or got into a fight. What happened? Was it someone you know? A mugger? Were you drunk at a bar or something?"

"No." Jerome looked affronted at my last suggestion, then his shoulders hunched. "It's nothing. I don't want to talk about it, okay?"

I sipped my coffee and studied him. He didn't meet my gaze, instead picking at his fingernail to keep his fidgeting hands occupied. His sandy-colored threads were twisted and snarled with his angst over whatever was bothering him. I wanted to push him harder for answers, but I didn't want to drive him away.

A barrier of secrets stood between us, and Jerome wasn't the only one contributing bricks to build it. What would he say if I told him about my past as March Feynman? For the first time, I wondered if my reveal should be sooner rather than later. Confessions begat confessions, and he might finally feel comfortable enough to share whatever darkness lurked under his calm exterior.

"Okay," I said. I scooted my chair around so I was closer to him, and reached out my hands to his threads. "Hold still so I can get these knots. Hey, guess what Amir did for me today?"

Jerome relaxed as I regaled him with my triumph of the morning. But when I gave his lips a chaste kiss goodbye with a lingering touch on his chest with my trailing fingers, the thought of revealing my own secrets wasn't far from my mind.

Although the promise of future work was on my horizon, money wasn't in my bank account yet. Rosemary was still willing to hire me for odds and ends at Cut Right, so I made my way there for a shift.

Joy and Miranda were working today, and both were with clients. Miranda looked relieved to see me.

"Can you grab the phone when it rings, please, Morgan?" She grabbed a comb and ran it through the elderly man's thinning locks in front of her.

"And sweep," Joy called out. She dabbed dye onto her client's head.

I tied an apron over my clothes, grabbed a broom, and started sweeping. When I neared Miranda, I caught her eye.

"Any luck with Shu?" I said.

Miranda shook her head. "I asked her about her thoughts on the Book, but I didn't get a definitive answer. I'm still not sure

32

what way she leans. I'll try again the next time I see her, though."

I nodded and continued to sweep. Feeling out Shu's loyalty wasn't an easy task.

"Try asking about her stance on utopia, whether there's another way to look at it," I said.

"She might see right through that." Miranda frowned and snipped near her customer's neck. "I don't know, Morgan."

"We need answers," I said. These tasks would be quicker if I did them, but every leader knew the power of delegation, as long as her followers understood their instructions. "Give it a try. Hopefully by tomorrow we have a new recruit."

Miranda twisted her mouth in concern, but she nodded and continued to trim the man's hair. I swept closer to Joy, and she finished her customer's dye with a flourish.

"There you are, Sherri. We'll let that set for a few minutes."

She tugged my elbow, and I followed her to the sink where she washed her hands.

"I spoke to Zakaria, one of the mothers. We had a nice long chat over tea." Joy grabbed a towel and rubbed her hands vigorously. "Apparently, Hazel is away hiking somewhere in the Kootenays, following a clue for the Thorn's whereabouts."

I frowned. What clue did Hazel have?

"Damn it. What if she finds it first?"

"I wouldn't worry too much about it." Joy threw her towel into the washing machine and rummaged on a top shelf for laundry detergent. "The elders are always hunting for the Thorn. I think Hazel just likes hiking, personally. They haven't found it yet."

"But they have the other two artifacts," I argued. Joy needed to take this threat more seriously. "If Hazel finds the Thorn, she has everything she needs to grow the Tree of Life and take all that power for herself."

Joy's face grew troubled. Miranda popped around the corner.

"Mr. Brody is finally gone," she said. "What's the news?"

"Hazel's looking for the Thorn." I tapped my fingers on the edge of the sink. "We need to know everything she knows. We need to read the Book of Souls. How do we get an elders' copy?"

Miranda and Joy glanced at each other.

"Not easily," Joy said finally. "The sisters have never even seen the mothers' version, and the mothers don't see the full text. Levels of initiation, right? I don't even know where they keep the original."

"Now that I think about it, I might know," Miranda said breathlessly. "I was helping Beatrice move furniture in her house one day, and she let slip something about the elders' amulet room. Apparently, it's not just a room, but a cabin in the field behind Agatha's orchard. It's heavily warded, and their most powerful amulets are stored there." Miranda's eyes shone. "What do you bet their Book of Souls is kept there? Where else would it be?"

I nodded slowly. "Yes, that makes sense. They don't need to refer to it often, and it's precious to them. They would only trust the magic of their amulets for protection, not a safety deposit box or anything like that."

"So, what are you saying, Morgan?" Joy looked fearful. "What do you want to do?"

"Steal the Book of Souls, of course," I said. "We need to know what's inside."

"But the wards." Miranda chewed her lip. "They will be powerful. And Joy and I can't get any amulets. Our head sister Filippa isn't letting us use any right now."

"Wait a minute." I stared at Miranda. "Are you saying you're still in the order? How did they let your actions at the Seed ceremony slide? You knocked out Wanda."

"I said you'd bewitched me." Miranda shrugged. "With your strange powers. They seemed to buy it."

"Well, not having amulets to use is a blow, but from what I

gather, the sisters' amulets aren't nearly as powerful as the elders', so no need to pine after them." I straightened my shirt. "We can rely on my elemental spirit instead. That will have to be enough. Miranda, will you show me the way tonight?"

Miranda gulped, her face pale. "Okay."

I rubbed my hands together. The car's vents blasted warm air, but Joy's borrowed car had seen better days, and it was having a hard time keeping up to the outside chill. With a few tweaks of air threads, I raised the temperature in the car to a pleasant level. Miranda flicked on the turn signal and veered off the highway.

"Let's run through the plan one more time," I said. "We park a short distance away and sneak around the house, through the orchard, and to the cabin. You remember where it is?"

"Yes, I think so." Miranda worried her bottom lip with her teeth and checked the rearview mirror.

I pursed my own lips. "I guess that will have to do. I'll push air toward us to hide our smell from Agatha's dog. If that doesn't work, I'll disable the wards while you placate the dog with treats. We go in, grab the book, and get out. Good?"

Miranda nodded, her forehead creased.

Our plan unfolded as expected for the first few minutes. We trekked along the road to Agatha's farmhouse nestled in dark fields, guided by the wavering beam of Miranda's flashlight. The large slab of bedrock that rose beside the house was a minor inconvenience, but we scaled it without issue and landed in Agatha's orchard on the other side.

The farmhouse windows were dark above its wraparound porch, and I sighed in relief. We had to be less careful with Agatha asleep. With light feet, we traipsed between rows of apples and pears. The trees' delicate blossoms glowed luminous in the darkness like the stars above, accompanied by a delicate scent of growth and life. It would have been magical and romantic had I been with someone else under different circumstances. As it was, my heart raced from adrenaline, and my mind barely registered the beauty before running through our plan again. A strong sense of déjà vu crept over me. The last time I was here, I'd been sneaking around in the dark, avoiding order members.

A booming bark echoed through the stillness of night. Miranda clutched my arm.

"Doug heard us," she hissed. "Keep going. I have treats ready."

"Agatha named her dog Doug?" I said in disbelief, but I joined Miranda in a jog eastward, away from the house. Doug's barking grew more frenzied and disconcertingly louder. I glanced at Miranda. "How close are we to this cabin?"

"Not far," she panted. "Keep going. I'll—oof!"

A massive black beast tackled Miranda to the ground. She gasped, her breath leaving her, while the dog accosted her with his slobbery mouth.

"Stop it, Doug." Miranda wrestled the animal back so she could sit up. "You're so wet. Yes, it's lovely to see you, too. Would you like a treat?"

At the word "treat", Doug sat on his haunches and waited, his tongue lolling and a goofy grin pulling his cheeks back. Miranda dug into her pocket and took out a wrinkly triangle. Doug grabbed the dried pig ear out of midair when she tossed it toward him and proceeded to gnaw the treat with gusto.

I took a deep, shuddering breath. "Why didn't you say he was so friendly?" I said to Miranda. "He scared the stuffing out of me."

"I wasn't sure how he'd react in the dark, but I forgot how much dogs use their noses instead of their eyes. He must have recognized me, even with your air tricks." She peered toward the house, barely visible through the trees. "I just hope he didn't wake up Agatha. Not that it would matter much. She wouldn't toddle out here in the dark, but her aide might."

"I don't see any lights," I said. "But let's keep moving and get this over with."

We continued eastward. Doug picked up his treat and followed us, his tail wagging and his teeth clacking against the pig ear in his mouth. After a minute, Miranda beckoned me forward.

"There it is," she said quietly. "Come on."

"Wait." I put out my hand to stop her. "Let me go first."

The tiny cabin, no bigger than a single room, was detailed to match the main farmhouse, clapboard siding, asphalt shingles, and all. I hardly spared a glance for its aesthetics, more concerned by the network of threads that draped over the door, slathered the windows, and spread across the grass.

Caelus emerged from my arm and surveyed the scene. "We've got our work cut out for us," he said.

Miranda jumped. "Who was that?" she hissed, her eyes wide. "Who's there?"

"I told you I'm possessed by an elemental spirit," I said absently, still examining the threads before us. "Miranda, meet Caelus. Caelus, Miranda. You won't be able to see him, only hear him."

"Okay," she said faintly, her eyes still searching the air around me for signs of the elemental.

"Yes, great to meet you," Caelus said without enthusiasm. "Now, Morgan, start by sweeping a path through the ground threads. They're only spillage from the cabin, not a trap or signal. It's the door threads we need to worry about."

I bent over double and brushed aside the multicolored strands that writhed over the ground in slow undulations. Slowly, I tracked a path to the door, Miranda following close behind me. Doug panted at her side, and she absentmindedly fed him another pig ear to keep him occupied.

When we stood in front of the door at last, Caelus and I

considered it. He reached out his insubstantial arm and touched a thread that was thicker than the others and glowed with a brighter light.

"Touch this one, this one, and this one," he instructed. "With intention. Calm them—they're full of energy ready to dissipate into anyone who barges into them."

"And me touching them won't activate them?" I eyed the glowing strands with trepidation. I had no desire to trigger whatever trap lay in wait.

"Not with enough intention." Caelus crossed his arms and looked at me expectantly. "Go on."

I took a deep breath then bent to grasp a thread with a firm grip. My brain focused with almost painful intensity on my task.

To my relief, no trap sprang on me. Instead, a pleasant fizzle of energy ran from my hand, through my body, and into the ground at my feet. Within seconds, the strand was dim and limp.

"Good," Caelus said. "Keep going."

I threw him a scathing glance but grabbed the next thread. One by one, the strands dimmed. Once they were all deactivated, I stepped back with a sigh of relief.

"It's clear," I said to Miranda. I walked forward to prove my point. Miranda followed me to the door of the cabin, and I turned the handle with more confidence than I felt.

The door creaked open. Inside was blissfully clear of wards, with only the usual threads of earth and air floating around the room.

"Is it safe?" Miranda whispered behind me.

"Come on in." I stepped aside, and she and Doug entered the small space.

The room gave off vibes of a sacred altar. Candles and glowing amulets lined two shelves that ran along walls on either side of us. Across from the door, a table covered with a cloth of delicate fabric held an ornate ring with a large ruby embedded in the center, although it was hardly visible through the thick layer of multicolored threads that surrounded it. The space was scented with the faint remains of incense.

"Have you ever been here before?" I asked Miranda.

"No, never." She gazed reverentially at the altar with its ring then shook her head. "It's hard to remember that all of this is a lie. It feels wrong in here, you know?"

She thumped her chest with her fist, and my heart squeezed in sympathy. Everything that Miranda had grown up believing had shattered around her, and she had to pick up the pieces and figure out a new configuration.

"It's still true," I said gently. "Some of it. The utopia you were promised might not come to pass, but the magic is real enough."

"Yes." Miranda released her breath and glanced at me swiftly. "I guess that's true. The amulets are real. Check out this hoard. The elders always have the best stuff." She picked up an old-fashioned key from the nearest shelf and read an index card accompanying it. "Wow, this one makes you super nimble, like a monkey-nimble."

I picked up another key and examined its card. I whistled. "This one gives the holder a huge confidence boost. That could be useful. Do you think they'd notice some amulets missing?"

"Maybe." Miranda shrugged. "But we're already planning on stealing the Book of Souls. In for a penny, in for a pound, right?"

"I like the way you think." I put the key in my pocket and looked longingly at the shelf full of thread-wrapped amulets before I shook my head to clear it of my desires. I had Caelus, who was better than a sack full of amulets. "Come on, let's find the Book and get out of here."

"Where do you propose looking?" Caelus asked. "Because I don't see any sign of it. I'd expect to see a thick cluster of threads, given the belief surrounding the Book, but there's nothing."

I looked around the room, but Caelus was right. Aside from the copious threads surrounding the ring on the altar, and the strands around each amulet, the room was devoid of obviously important books.

"I don't know." Miranda bit her lip. "If it's not here, I don't know where else to look. Maybe Agatha has it in her house, but I thought here would be the best place for it."

I dropped to my hands and knees and examined the floor for loose floorboards or hidden hatches where someone could hide the Book. Doug snuffled closer to me. He chuffed, and I looked at him. "What's up, Doug?"

He chuffed again, then snuffled over to a corner of the room. With his paw, he scrabbled at the wall. Miranda and I glanced at each other, then I crawled over to Doug.

"What did you find, boy?" I ran my fingers over the wall where he had pawed, and Miranda illuminated the spot with her flashlight. My finger hitched on an almost invisible metal loop embedded in the wall. I pulled at it in triumph, and a small door fell open toward me.

Threads of every color spilled out. They lit the small recess in the wall and outlined a leatherbound book.

"The Book of Souls," Miranda whispered. "The real one."

"Good boy," I said to Doug. The dog must have seen Agatha take the Book from its cubby in the past. My hands reached out and carefully grasped either side of the Book. I lifted it out gingerly.

"It's fine," Caelus said. "The only wards were on the door. They never expected intruders to get this far."

I flipped the Book open. A waft of old pages drifted past my nose, and I fought a sneeze. The title page was familiar— it featured in both the sisters' and the mothers' copies—but this was clearly the original. I flipped the pages, then I frowned and held the Book out to Miranda.

"I forgot, it's all in Latin," I said. "Mine's too rusty. How's yours?"

"We all learn Latin from childhood." Miranda took the Book with careful hands as if she were handling a newborn baby. She flipped pages until a point two-thirds of the way through and shone her flashlight at it. "Here, this is the elders' section. I've never seen it before. Rosemary showed me the mothers' part."

"Well, what does this page say?" Caelus jittered on my arm with impatience.

Miranda jumped at his voice but continued to read. "Give me a minute. Just because I know how to read Latin doesn't mean I'm quick at it."

Caelus and I allowed Miranda to mouth the words soundlessly to herself for a few minutes. He exchanged a loaded glance with me.

"How's it going?" I said to Miranda, trying to keep my tone pleasant. I was as impatient as Caelus, but Miranda didn't need any more pressure.

"Okay, I think I've got this part." Miranda brushed hair out of her eyes. She looked at me with a worried expression. "It's not good. Listen to this.

"*The release of Spirit will change the world as we know it. The upheaval that will follow is terrible but necessary. For Spirit must be reborn, and no birth is without pain. Mountains will rise, rivers will flood, winds will howl, and the hot veins of Earth will flow in the valleys. The Tree of Life will grow through the destruction, and when it is mature, Spirit will rise and a new day will dawn for those who live to see it. Only those who contribute blood to the Thorn will live forever. The rest must take their chances.*"

CHAPTER V

Miranda and I stared at each other, and Caelus drifted closer to me.

"I had no idea," Caelus said softly. "Morgan, this goes against everything I'm trying to do. Think of the imbalance in the elements this will cause. We can't let this happen."

My stomach churned as I imagined the promised destruction. What were the odds that I would be a survivor?

"No, we can't." I swallowed past the lump of fear in my throat. I'd been helping find artifacts mainly for Caelus' sake, although keeping power out of the head mother Thea Diamanto's hands had been a close second. But I'd never imagined anything like this.

I might not be the most virtuous person in the world, but I couldn't stand by and allow the elders to bring an apocalypse. The rest of the world was oblivious. It was up to me, Caelus and our ragtag group of sisters to take on the might of the order before they destroyed everything.

"I had no idea." Miranda's face was white even in the darkness of the cabin. "This is worse than I'd feared. And are the elders planning on becoming immortal? Is that one of the things they've been hiding from us?"

Doug padded outside while Miranda and I stared at each other. After a moment, his distant woof of greeting startled me out of my paralysis.

"Someone's coming," I hissed. "Quick, get out of the cabin."

Miranda raced to the door with me close behind her. I closed the door as quietly as I could then followed Miranda around the back of the cabin. We flattened ourselves against the wall and tried to quiet our breathing. Miranda clutched the Book of Souls against her heaving chest.

"Was your trip successful?" Beatrice's soft voice carried

over the silent grass.

"Not successful enough." Hazel's strident tone whipped across my ears. "Obviously. But at least I've narrowed it down to southern British Columbia."

"Did you tell Agatha yet?"

Hazel scoffed. "You know she's next to useless these days. Her days as a helpful pawn are over. Even if we find the Thorn before she dies, I don't know if I'll bother granting her immortality. Let her pass over in peace. She's too wrapped up in the utopia nonsense, anyway, like the younger ones. She used to be more pragmatic. Her mind must be going."

"Why is Doug running around at night?" Panting greeted this remark. Beatrice must be rubbing Doug's head. "It's late, and there might be wild animals out."

"Like I said, her mind's going. Go on, Doug. Back to the house."

Padding footsteps sounded, but to my horror, they increased in volume. Doug's black head peeked around the corner. He gave a happy bark.

"Move," I breathed to Miranda. She gave Doug one terrified glance before bolting after me in the opposite direction. Doug gave a playful bark and leaped alongside us.

"Hey!" Hazel shouted out. "Who's there? Show yourselves!"

I threw a blast of wind behind me then sprinted down an alley of trees. Shouts grew in intensity as both women gave chase, but we were younger and had the element of surprise.

"Miranda," Hazel shouted. "Morgan. I see you both. You won't get away with this."

"Doug," Miranda gasped. "Go home."

Doug shot her a reproachful glance but veered away to return to the other women. When I glanced back, he was leaping up at the two with exuberant barks. Whether he intended it or not, he slowed our pursuers enough for us to scramble over the bedrock and make our escape.

Back at the car, Miranda shoved keys in the ignition and tore away from the side of the road with a spray of gravel.

"Damn it," she said, her voice wavering with emotion. "They saw us."

"We can't stay in the open anymore," I said, my brain whirling through the repercussions of tonight's fiasco. "But we can't stop thwarting them. We're on the run, now, whether we like it or not."

"At least we know the truth." Miranda patted the Book of Souls in her lap with a shaky hand.

"And," I said with steely resolve hardening my voice. "We will do whatever we need to do to stop it."

"They'll be looking for us now," I said to Miranda when she pulled in front of my condo. "You're out of the order, that's for sure. What would they do to you, do you think?"

"I don't know." Miranda's voice edged into the realm of panic.

"We need to lay low," I said. "The elders will be coming after us. Stay at your place at your own risk."

"Where do we go?"

I took a deep breath, unsure what to say but knowing I needed to take the reins here. "Pack your things, then meet me behind the coffeeshop in an hour. I'll have something figured out by then, okay?"

Miranda nodded, the speed of her jittery head reminding me of Beaky's bobbing neck.

"I'll take the Book of Souls for safekeeping." I scooped the Book under my arm. "Caelus will protect it."

"Okay," Miranda said with a tremble in her voice. I patted her on the arm then stepped out with my hood up. When she zoomed off, I sighed.

"That grace period didn't last long," Caelus said. "I thought we'd have all this time to leisurely investigate the Thorn's location."

"At least we have the Book of Souls now. But, I agree, I'd hoped for longer." I stared up at my condo while I walked to the front door. "What do you think? Can we ward this place enough to keep it safe from Hazel and Beatrice, or do we need to run?"

Caelus pursed his lips and squished them to one side. "I don't know how powerful the elders are. Some of the amulets pack a punch. And the problem is, even if we can ward the condo—which we should be able to, given that I'm an elemental and they are only using human-made amulets—what happens when you try to leave and they're waiting for you in an ambush? We can't ward the entire neighborhood."

"That's true." My heart sank at the thought of leaving my condo. It was my first home as Morgan Feynman, and it held a special place in my heart. I knew it couldn't be mine forever—eventually, March's estate would be settled, and someone would come knocking to sell the holding—but I'd thought I would have longer. "Okay, run it is. But where?"

Caelus was silent while I slid my key in the door and entered my condo. I didn't have much to pack, just some clothes, toiletries, and a few cans of food that might come in handy, and it wasn't long before my backpack was full and ready by the door. I tried to push down my feelings of regret, but they kept welling up.

"Call the others," Caelus said finally. "Maybe they have somewhere to stay."

With one last look at my condo, I closed the door behind us.

By the time Miranda slunk into the alley behind Sacred Grounds coffeeshop, Joy and Amanda had also arrived, and the three of us were waiting for her.

"Joy!" Miranda flung her arms around her sisters. "Amanda. Did Morgan tell you what happened? It was awful. Now I have a target on my back."

"Yeah, you do," Joy said in an unusually somber tone. She held up her phone with a message app glowing on the screen. "We've all been warned. We have orders to alert Hazel if we see you. You need to watch your backs."

Miranda's lip trembled, and she dashed away tears from her eyes.

"What's happening to my life?" she mumbled.

"It's okay." Amanda gave her another squeeze.

Joy tucked her phone back into her pocket. "Morgan called and asked if I have somewhere you can stay, and I totally do. I'm housesitting for my paternal grandparents. They live just down the road. No one would suspect that location. There are spare bedrooms for you both."

"And you're okay with harboring two fugitives?" I asked.

Joy nodded, her eyes hard. "If I had doubts before, I don't have any now. They want to take you in for 'rehabilitation'. What the hell does that mean? Nothing good, I can guess. No, we need the truth, and that's all you two were looking for. We're in this together, now."

I clasped her shoulder briefly, heartened by her loyalty. Amanda gave me a reassuring nod.

"Contact with the order is on you two, now," I said. "If you want to bring Shu into the fold, do so very carefully. I don't think either Miranda or I want to be rehabilitated."

Miranda shook her head until hair whipped her face.

"Come on, the car's this way," Joy said. "Make sure your hoods are up. And don't greet any order member you might see on the street, especially Denise and Wanda. They're both very pro-order at the moment."

Amanda left for her home, and Joy drove us to a two-level house with a pale stone façade and windows that followed the shape of the roof. Tall trees shaded the front yard and provided a sense of privacy. I sighed in relief. If I had to be on the run, I could think of worse hideouts.

"This will do nicely," I said aloud. My mouth opened in a jaw-cracking yawn. "Please, lead me to a bed."

Joy chuckled, the sound appealing after the intensity of our evening so far, and led us into the house. Up the carpeted stairs, past framed photographs of Joy and her family, Joy pointed at a room on the left.

"That's yours, Morgan. Sleep tight."

I entered the room, but Caelus popped out of my arm immediately after.

"Aren't we going to ward the house?" he asked. "Hazel is after you. We don't want her finding this place."

"Yes, you're right." I yawned and dragged myself downstairs. Once outside, I picked up my hands.

"Remind me what to do again," I said to Caelus. "It was a month ago that we did my condo."

Caelus directed my movements, and I wove threads over the front door and all the windows. With any luck—unless Hazel had amulets for this—only the people we invited in would be able to enter.

I climbed the stairs with heavy feet once finished. Exhaustion hit me like a blow to the head as soon as the door closed behind me. I dropped my backpack, shrugged off my coat, and crawled into bed fully dressed. I was unconscious seconds later.

The sky was still dark when I awoke, but my mind immediately flicked into top gear. After a minute of attempting to calm my racing heart and whirling mind, I cursed and sat up. There was no way I would get back to sleep now. Elders, amulets, and artifacts chased around my head like puppies after their own tails.

I picked up my phone and checked the time. It was five in the morning. I wanted to talk to someone, get the thoughts out of my head and into someone else's, but Miranda and Joy would likely still be asleep. Everyone sensible was asleep at five in the morning.

Except one. I propped my pillow against the wall and leaned against it, eager to hear Jerome's voice. He would be at the bakery at this time, kneading dough and measuring ingredients for scones. My fingers flew over my phone, summoning him.

"Morgan?" Jerome's deep voice relaxed something in my core, and I almost wondered if I could get back to sleep if he would keep talking to me over the phone while I closed my eyes. Some whirring machine thumped in the background. "Are you okay? It's early for you."

"Sort of. I'm not hurt. Miranda and I stole the Book of Souls last night, and the elders saw us." I settled into my pillow more comfortably. "Now we're on the run. The order has been told to bring us in. Who knows what they have planned for us? I'd rather not be mind-controlled or whatever else they could manage."

"What?" Jerome's voice sharpened. "Are you in danger? This is ridiculous. At what point do you give up and go to the police?"

I shuddered. I couldn't involve the police. My identity was too precarious for investigation, and how would I explain Caelus and amulets and everything unexplainable? It would sound ridiculous to an uninitiated cop, and my case would be weak without that information.

"No cops," I said.

"Okay." Jerome sounded oddly relieved. "Then, what? Do

you have somewhere to go? Where are you now? You can stay at my place if you need somewhere to crash.”

My stomach flopped pleasurably. I wasn’t ready to stay at Jerome’s place, but I wasn’t far from it. But I didn’t want this crisis to force something that was already progressing so beautifully. I was touched that he’d offered, though.

“That’s very sweet of you,” I said. “But I’m staying at Joy’s place. She’s housesitting, so it’s not an obvious place to look.”

“Can you give me the address?” he said. The whirring noise in the background switched off. “I can come over right after work to see you, bring you some food, maybe.”

“I’ll text you.” I snuggled down into the pillow, feeling sleepy again, and an odd mix of contented and worried. I blurted out, “I miss you.”

Where had that come from? I bit my tongue, but Jerome’s voice had a smile in it when he responded.

“I’ll be there as soon as I can.”

I hung up, feeling strangely comforted. Maybe I could sleep a little longer, after all.

I slept for another hour. When I awoke and padded downstairs in a fresh change of clothes, Miranda was sitting at the kitchen table amid the wreckage of a breakfast of toast crumbs. She gripped a mug of tea, untasted, and the sides of her mouth drooped. She dragged listless eyes upward when I entered.

“Joy’s getting dressed,” she said, her voice flat. “The others will be here before they go to work.”

“I know you feel low about all this.” I crossed the room and sank into the chair next to Miranda’s. “But this will pass, and you’ll be glad your eyes were opened to the truth.”

“It’s not that. Well, okay, it partly is. But what am I supposed to do now? Do I go to my classes at the university,

49

or am I being watched? Can I go to work at Cut Right? Am I stuck in this house forever?”

Miranda’s voice rose with every question. I reminded myself that she was still only nineteen and prone to dramatism. Having more years under my belt gave me greater perspective.

“No, you probably shouldn’t go to work,” I said firmly. Miranda slumped ever further in her chair. “The elders no doubt know your schedule, and they would use that opportunity to grab you.” I pierced her with an intent look. “You won’t be stuck in this house forever. I recommend you dig out your textbooks and study during your absenteeism.”

“What’s the point?” Miranda said bitterly. “Why am I even taking archaeology classes, anyway? It was all for the order. Everything I’ve done has always been for the order. I don’t even like history. My favorite class in high school was chemistry. What am I supposed to do now?”

This was a heavier conversation than I was prepared for before coffee, but I did my best.

“You’re young, and you have plenty of time to figure out what to do with your life. In fact, all this turmoil is a good thing. Once you rise out of it, you’ll be able to choose your own path in life without reference to the order. You want to study chemistry? Now you can make it happen. Your life is yours to direct.”

Miranda nodded slowly, her face relaxing from its previous frown. She sipped her tea with a thoughtful expression.

I stood, content that I’d smoothed over Miranda’s dilemma for now, and rummaged in cupboards for coffee. The best I found was some instant powder. My lip curled, but I grabbed it anyway and put the kettle on to boil. March wouldn’t have touched the stuff, but Morgan—well, Morgan would take what she could get. Reluctantly.

Three sips into my anemic mug of coffee, there was a knock at the door. Miranda and I stared at each other. My heart pounded. Had the elders arrived already?

CHAPTER VI

"It's probably Amanda," Miranda said faintly. "Probably. We should check."

She didn't move, so I tiptoed to the front door and peered out the peephole. Amanda's ginger ponytail and Shu's sleek black hair calmed my heart to a manageable speed, and I flung the door wide.

"Quickly," I said, glancing at the street. "Who knows who might be watching."

They scuttled in. A rust-colored pigeon cooed at me, and I stared.

"Beaky?" I whispered. "Good to see you. I'll bring bread out soon, I promise."

I shut the door behind me, more pleased that I cared to admit that Beaky had followed me to our hideout. Joy clattered down the stairs, her fingers fumbling at her ears with a pair of large hoop earrings.

"What's going on?" Shu gasped. "We've been told to bring you to Hazel, no questions asked. What did you do?" She held up her hand as if to stop any objections. "Just so we're clear, I am totally on your side. The order shouldn't have the artifacts, that's clear."

"Wait until you hear what we found in the Elders' Book of Souls." I fetched the book from the kitchen and brought it to the entryway then read them the relevant section.

"Widescale destruction?" Joy whispered. She exchanged a horrified glance with Shu. "Oh, Morgan, I might be with you on getting rid of the artifacts after all."

"This feels too close to the truth to be denied," Shu said. "Miranda told me about the mothers being promised power when the artifacts are joined, and I confirmed it with my own mother, who's one of them."

"What did you tell her?" Joy put her hands on her hips and

glared at Shu. "We need to keep this a secret from them. I don't care if she's related to you, this is too important to mess up."

"Relax," Shu shot her own glare back at her sister. "Honestly, how stupid do you think I am? I was careful." She turned to me. "Anyway, I'm on board. However you're planning to keep the artifacts out of the hands of the mothers and elders, I'm in."

"Me too," Amanda said eagerly. "If we're not getting the utopia we're promised, I don't see why the others should get unlimited powers. That's not fair at all."

Amanda's petulant words reminded me again how young some of my new team were, and I sighed inwardly. They needed a firm guiding hand. It was lucky I was here.

"I'm glad to have you," I said warmly. "Every order member with us means one less against us. Every one of you can contribute to the important work of finding the Thorn, recovering the Leaf and Seed, and putting the order off our scent."

As a woman, they puffed up with importance and pride.

"What can I do?" Shu said.

"You, Amanda, and Joy are still part of the order." I glanced at each one in turn. "I need you to ask how the search for the Thorn is progressing and what they plan for Miranda and me. In addition, you can plant information for us. Say you saw me getting on a bus heading east, or Miranda texted to say she's going to visit family out of town. Get creative. The idea is to lead the others on a wild goose chase while we sit tight here."

"We can do that," Joy said, and the others nodded. "Come on, girls, let's go."

The three traipsed out of the house. When the front door closed, I wandered back into the kitchen, where Miranda had remained during our brief meeting.

"If you're not planning to study," I said to her. "We have a rather obscure book in need of translation."

Miranda pulled a Latin dictionary out of her backpack and wiped the table clean of crumbs. The prospect of translation seemed to have galvanized her, as I'd suspected it would. I ran into the hall for the Book of Souls.

I stopped at the console table where the Book lay. My shift at the women's center where I volunteered was supposed to be today. Now that Hazel and the order were after me, it wouldn't be safe for me or for the center if I showed up. With a heavy heart, I called them and expressed my apologies to Greta, the volunteer coordinator.

When I returned to the kitchen, Miranda was sitting at the ready with a pencil and paper before her and her dictionary on the side.

"Perfect," I said, sitting next to her. "How about you read the translation aloud, and I write it down for you?"

Miranda bit her lip in thought. "Okay," she said at last. "I'll be slow, but that should work. Here we go.

"To create the illusion of your opponent feeling heavier than they should, first take powdered root of the marshmallow plant and sprinkle it over your chosen object. Then pour water in a circle around the object in a counterclockwise direction. Hum deeply for a full minute while concentrating on your goal, then say the trigger word aloud. With enough focus, an amulet will be made."

"Fascinating," I said, my mind whirling. "Nothing about Spirit and the Thorn, but excellent all the same."

"Does this mean we can make our own amulets?" Miranda stared at me, my own gleam of acquisition reflected in her eyes.

"That's my understanding." I flipped the page over and glanced at the illustrations. These, too, showed images of rings and necklaces surrounded by candles, assorted strange ingredients, and small animals. My body tensed with excitement. Could we level the playing field against the elders with a few simple creations?

Caelus emerged from my arm and leaned over Miranda's shoulder.

"Why do I know nothing of Spirit?" he said plaintively.

Miranda jumped and put her hand to her heart.

"Caelus?" she said. "Is that you?"

"Nope, I'm the other disembodied voice in the room." Only I could see Caelus' thready eyes roll. "Yes, it's me."

"What do you think of all this?" Miranda waved at the Book.

Caelus gave me a look that spoke volumes. "Well, so nice of you to ask. Morgan hasn't bothered yet, even though I'm the most qualified entity in the room."

"You just finished saying you don't know anything about Spirit," I said.

Caelus crossed his arms. "I'm still the most qualified. But to answer your question, Miranda, I think it is most intriguing, but I will be happy to see the artifacts destroyed with no chance of the turmoil predicted. Elemental things should stay in the elemental plane."

Miranda looked thoughtful and she nodded. Then her eyes flicked over the text, and her lips moved soundlessly.

"These instructions look really tricky." She pointed at an illustration. "Not only do we need these weird spices and stuff, we have to prepare them in the perfect way and do the right actions over them. And we have to truly believe in what we're doing. I don't think it's possible." She slumped with her head propped on her hand, every thread drooping with despair.

"All solvable," I said with a wave of my hand. If we had the instructions, everything else could be managed. "Is the rest of the Book of Souls essentially a recipe book?"

"Looks like it." Miranda flipped through the pages listlessly. "Yeah, look at this one that makes someone heavier.

The sisters have that one. And this one that grows your hair out. Ooo, and one that slows your opponent's mind."

"I like the sound of that one." I pulled a fresh sheet of paper toward me. "A dumbing spell. Tell me the ingredients again. I'll go shopping. Might as well bring guns to a gun fight, right?"

Miranda grinned weakly despite her despondency and ran her finger down the list.

Miranda and I translated for hours. By the end, she was bleary from poring over the ancient Latin text, and I had a stack of recipes for amulets of all sorts, like ones for boosting confidence, turning someone temporarily blind, and making them believe they were an animal.

"I saw an exercise bike downstairs." Miranda stood and stretched. "I need to move. See you later."

I nodded and tidied up our work after she'd gone. My stomach rumbled. We'd grabbed some more toast for lunch, but we really needed groceries. Tomorrow, I decided. I would wear sunglasses and a hood and brave the store tomorrow.

Caelus floated in front of my face with an expectant expression. "When's the last time you practiced my air powers? You're going to get rusty, and now is not the time to slip up. Hazel could be around any corner, and your fumbling fingers won't have the muscle memory to react."

"Such little faith in my abilities." I glared at Caelus. "I'm as ready as ever. But more practice couldn't hurt. I wonder how private the backyard is."

I wandered out the back porch and down the patio stairs. The tiny yard was fenced with a spreading copper beech in the middle which filled the yard with shade. Even if the neighbors could see past its sweeping bare branches, no one stirred in the windows of neighboring houses on this workday.

The clouds threatened rain, but they hadn't delivered yet. I zipped my coat up to my neck and rubbed my hands.

"What should we try first?" I said to Caelus. "Air balls? Fog? Tornado?"

"You're pretty wobbly with the whole flying thing." Caelus looked me up and down with a critical eye. "The few times you've tried, you looked like a bird who's eaten too many fermented berries."

"That's what I love about you." I gathered silver threads in my hands in preparation. "Always so full of compliments. You really know how to encourage."

"It seems to work for you. Now, quit stalling. What if Hazel were sneaking up on you right now?"

I willed myself not to glance behind me at Caelus' words. It was too easy to indulge in paranoia. Better to practice my skills and go on the offensive if someone attacked.

When the threads in my hands were correctly oriented, I pulled gently upward. With a stomach-dropping jolt, my feet left the ground. Buoyed by the billowing cloud of air under my body, I drifted among branches of the copper beech.

"Watch out for that one," Caelus commented. "That would hurt."

For practice, I maneuvered myself into a seated position on the branch Caelus had warned me about and released the air threads. My face cracked open in a wide grin.

"That was smooth," I said to Caelus with pride. "Look how high we are."

I glanced down and swallowed. We were very high indeed.

Caelus chuckled. "Afraid of heights? I can't say I understand the notion. Air elementals are always midair."

"Think about what would happen to our squishy body if it fell from this height, then talk to me about fear."

Caelus glanced at the ground then at me in consideration.

"Okay, I get it," he said finally. "Our body is pretty squishy."

I practiced floating around the tree branches for another half hour, fast and slow, until I was confident that my control was excellent. Caelus was right—if I wanted to stay ahead of Hazel, I needed to be on top of my game. She might have amulets, but I had air powers.

I drifted to the ground and let the grass take my weight. My phone buzzed, and I picked it up with a smile.

"Hi, Jerome."

"I know it's early, but are you up for some takeout dinner at my place?" He paused. "Wait, should you be out? Maybe I should come to yours like I promised before."

"No, it's fine." I stood and stretched. "I'll be careful. I need to get out for a bit before I go crazy. I'll be there shortly."

I couldn't help the grin that crossed my face as I walked inside with light feet and downstairs to find Miranda. I was as bad as a teenager. Was it the influence of my younger body or the girls I hung around? Oh, well. If I looked twenty-something, I might as well embrace all aspects of it.

"I'm going to Jerome's for dinner," I said to a red-faced Miranda.

She stopped pedaling and stared at me. "You're going out? Are you nuts?"

"I'll keep my hood up. Vancouver's a big city, no one will look twice at me." I retreated before Miranda could voice any other objections.

I walked swiftly through the still-bright streets. The sun was low in the sky, and it swept rays of orange fire between buildings and turned white blossoms into fiery candles.

Jerome's apartment block could have used a little love on the dirty stucco and wooden shingles that covered the walls in an alternating pattern, but at least each apartment had a large balcony. I buzzed his number, and a second later, the door clicked open. When I walked down the first-floor hall, that fusty smell of an unaired apartment hall clinging to the dingy carpeting, a door on my left swung open.

"Morgan." Jerome grinned at me from his open apartment door, although creases of worry clung to his eyes. "Come on in. It's not much, but there are no elders here."

I entered Jerome's apartment for the first time, intensely curious about his abode. It was a typical seventies build and hadn't been updated much since. Old linoleum covered the kitchen floor, and the living room carpet had seen better days. His furniture looked old but clean and cared-for. I touched his arm for no better reason than I wanted to.

"Thanks for having me over."

"Hope you don't mind the early dinner." He took my coat and hung it on the door handle. "That's what you get for dating a baker. I'm starving by four."

"What are we having?" I wandered into the tiny kitchen and peered in a bag. The scent of Southeast Asian spices wafted into my nose.

"Thai. I hope that's okay. I'm not the greatest cook, so I thought takeout was safest."

I stared at him. "You cook for a living."

"I bake," he corrected me with a twitch of his mouth. "Not cook. Unless you want bread and lemon tarts for dinner…"

"Well, that wouldn't be the end of the world." I sniffed the bag again. "But this smells lovely. Let's eat."

Jerome grabbed plates and cutlery, then we sat on his couch in the living room and balanced our food in our laps. He had a small table, but I suspected the couch was more comfortable. Jerome was good company, as usual, but I didn't need to see the tight knots in his threads to know that he was anxious about something.

"Are you going to tell me what's wrong?" I said when I couldn't contain my curiosity anymore. "You're worried about something. It's not me, is it?"

Jerome's threads didn't react how I would have expected them to if he were concerned about me. It must have been something else.

"No, no." Jerome swallowed his bite but didn't meet my eyes. "I'm fine."

I narrowed my eyes at him but didn't prod further. A flapping at the window ledge distracted me.

"What's that bird doing?" Jerome stood to get a better look. I peered over the couch, then I laughed aloud.

"That's Beaky. What is she doing here?" I shook my head in wonder. "I swear she's following me."

Jerome chuckled. "I've never heard of a pet pigeon before. Here, do you think she'd like some rice?"

He scooped a few grains from his almost empty plate and walked over to the window. Beaky fluttered away from the opening, but she didn't go far. Jerome carefully poured the rice onto the ledge and closed the window.

"Pet pigeon or guardian bird," I said. "She's helped me out before. We have a strange relationship, but it works for me."

I placed my plate on the table, and Jerome sat next to me, a little closer this time, close enough to feel his body heat. My body stirred with desire, and I finally allowed it to without pushing down the feelings. My fingers reached up and trailed down his neck, and he shivered. His honey-colored eyes gazed into mine with an unspoken question.

I leaned forward—slowly but without hesitation—and met his approaching lips with mine. His mouth was soft at first and tasted of coconut and spice. Then his questioning touch grew surer. His hand reached for my thigh and ran up my leg to my hip. I pushed into him, my palm against the hard planes of his chest. My mind grew blank, filled only with my desire to get closer to Jerome.

"This is getting too much for me," Caelus said beside us.

CHAPTER VII

Jerome jumped, and his hand flew off me. I breathed hard, trying to regain my composure to speak.

"You couldn't have just kept quiet in there?" I said unsteadily.

"The sensations were intriguing, at first. Then it just became awkward and boring. Don't you two have something more interesting to do?"

I gripped my head and a growl of frustration slipped out.

"Can't you just—" I looked wildly around the room for a solution. My gaze landed on Beaky outside the window, and a ray of hope lit my mind. "Caelus. Transfer to Beaky for a bit, would you?"

"You want me to get in the rat-bird?" Caelus' frown was magnificent, but I didn't have the patience to argue with him.

"Yes. Now. She'll be more interesting than us."

I jumped to the window and opened it with a cluck for Beaky. With a final grumble, Caelus gathered his threads and floated away from my body with my hearty encouragement. As he left, my thread-vision faded. I blinked hard a few times. It was disconcerting to turn off one of my senses.

"So, he's gone?" Jerome looked wary but hopeful.

I sat on the couch again then smiled seductively and looked up at him through my eyelashes.

"Yes. Now, shall we continue where we left off, or do you want to play cards?"

Jerome chuckled then swooped down at me. I laughed and met his eager mouth with my own.

Jerome's hands were everywhere, and I couldn't keep my own off him. His lips ran down my neck, and I sighed in pleasure. How long had it been since I'd been touched like this? How much longer since I'd felt overwhelming, gut-clenching desire?

A door slammed in the hallway, and Jerome jumped. He glanced toward the front door. I pulled his face back toward mine.

"It's just a neighbor," I whispered. "Don't stop."

Jerome kissed my lips again, but his hands weren't as sure and eager as before. His attention was on listening for further noises, and I didn't need to see his threads to know his were on high alert. What was he worried about? What was he hiding?

Finally, I pushed him away and wriggled upright. He stared at me in confusion.

"We can continue this later," I said. "When you're not so distracted. I want to be the center of your attention, and I don't like to share."

I smiled to soften my words, but Jerome looked away and swallowed.

"I'm sorry. It's just—" He paused. "You're right, I'm distracted. I'm sorry."

I waited, but whatever Jerome was distracted by, he wasn't spilling the beans. I sighed.

"I guess I should get out of your hair. Four in the morning will be here before you know it."

Jerome's shoulders slumped, but he didn't try to stop me. I stood and walked to my coat.

"Thanks for dinner." I glanced at Jerome, and he stared back with conflicted eyes. "And whenever you want to talk, I'm ready to listen."

The evening air was brisk now that the sun had set. I pulled my hood up over my hair, missing Caelus and his thread-vision. I felt naked and vulnerable without him. Hopefully, Hazel didn't have her sights on me tonight. I had little to defend myself with except a few self-defense moves and my running speed.

A bird flapped overhead, then the world blossomed with colorful threads. I grinned.

"Caelus, you're back."

"What are you doing out here?" Caelus' thread-form emerged from my arm. He frowned. "I thought humans liked to do their mating rituals for longer than that."

I rolled my eyes at him, both exasperated and amused. "Yes, we generally do. But Jerome was distracted by whatever is bothering him, and I don't like to take second place. I wish he would tell me what he's hiding."

"Just like you've told him about your body-switching past?" Caelus crossed his arms and looked at me with a raised eyebrow. I swatted his threads, and he briefly dissolved around my hand.

"Maybe I will soon."

"Anyway, enough about your mysterious love life." Caelus cleared his throat, an affectation to gather attention. "Beaky and I went back to your condo. We had to go somewhere, and Beaky is still fond of your balcony even though you're not there anymore. Guess who we saw?"

The last of my amorous desires melted away, replaced by a cold, trickling sensation down my back.

"Hazel."

"The one and the same." Caelus twirled a loose thread around his finger. "She was looking for you, for clues to where you've gone, I don't know. She trashed the place, turned it upside down searching. There's even a hole in the wall, now. She already has the artifacts, but maybe she was hoping for more. She left an amulet at the front door. A trap, maybe? The condo definitely isn't safe to go back to, that's for sure."

I sighed. This evening hadn't shaped up quite the way I'd hoped.

I slept poorly, and when I did sleep, my dreams alternated between sexy hands running up and down my body, and a shadowy figure stalking me through alleys. I awoke distinctly unrested and wandered downstairs in search of coffee.

Joy was bustling in the kitchen, and she'd managed to find an actual coffeemaker. I nearly kissed her.

"You're a lifesaver," I said, gratefully accepting a mug of steaming drink. "Are you off to work this morning?"

"We're short-staffed since both you and Miranda can't come in." She spread peanut butter on her toast. "Rosemary's hoping to hire someone for the short-term, but she hasn't had any luck so far. Oh." Joy turned to face me. "I found out what the elders intend for you two. It'll be a comprehensive memory wipe. I don't know how far back it will go. Will you remember us at all? Will Miranda go back to following the order? The elders have a very strong amulet, but I don't know how precise it is."

I sipped my coffee, highly unsettled by the notion of my brain being tampered with.

"I'll have to make sure not to get caught," I said lightly. "I rather like my memories where they are."

Joy tapped her foot, then she put her knife down with a decided air.

"I can't do this anymore," she burst out. "I can't toe the party line. The order is going too far. Hazel has always been bossy, but now she's a tyrant. She's acting like we're soldiers in a war, and questions are not only not allowed, but punished. I'm afraid of what will happen if she finds out that I'm lying to the order. I'm going to break away from them."

"No." It was a terrible idea, and I outlined why for Joy. "Trust me, being on the run isn't as glamorous as it sounds, and it comes with its own suite of anxieties. Do you want the threat of a mind-wipe dangling over you? Anyway, you're far more valuable as an inside woman than stuck here in the house with us. The faster we get intel and find the artifacts, the faster this will all be over."

Joy chewed her lip. "I don't know," she argued. "I'm a

terrible liar. They'll find me out one day."

"You're doing great." I patted her on the shoulder. Joy might resist my directives, but it was for the best that she followed them. Someone needed to take the reins of our ragtag group, and that meant making the hard decisions that no one else wanted to do. "Keep it up. In the order is the best place for you right now."

"I guess." She sighed explosively then turned back to her toast. "I hope we find the Thorn soon. I'll ask around today about the Leaf and Seed."

Joy left without her customary verve, but she was still paying lip service to the order, which was in our best interest. Miranda was still sleeping, so I took the opportunity to work on my business. After Amir's help, I now had three new paying clients to deliver plans to. I would work until the specialty grocery store opened, then I would buy the final ingredients to make amulets this afternoon. Having a plan to execute filled me with resolve, and I bent over my papers on the kitchen table with determination.

Miranda drifted into the kitchen midway through the morning, but I was deep in a conversation with one of the shop owners on the phone and only nodded my greeting to her. I could conduct most of my business on paper, online, and over the phone, but I finally hit a snag.

"I'll need to see your store," I said finally, after a few minutes of discussion with the owner of a children's toy shop. "I'll visit this afternoon."

We said our goodbyes and I hung up. My stomach churned, but the exposure was unavoidable. Caelus emerged from my arm.

"You need to go to the store to get our amulet ingredients anyway," he reminded me. "I'll watch your back."

"You're right." I stood and gathered my papers. "The order can't be everywhere at once. This is no big deal. It's nothing that a good pair of sunglasses won't solve."

Despite my confident words, my palms were sweating when I left the safety of Joy's grandparents' house. Every passerby might be an order member, and I scrutinized each one. Luckily, I knew all the order members by sight now, and my heart calmed a little at each unfamiliar face I passed. Caelus perched on my shoulder and gazed around ceaselessly for signs of familiar threads, and I felt better knowing that two pairs of eyes were watching for trouble.

My visit to the toy store passed without incident, and I left with assurances to the owner that I would have a plan for her by the end of the week.

I entered the specialty grocery with a sigh of relief. This was my final stop, then I could retreat to the house and begin preparations for making an amulet. My skin prickled with excitement. I'd made amulets in my previous life as a leader of a clandestine occult organization, but mine had been weak and unfocused compared to the order's. If the elders were coming after us, I wanted as much power as I could, if only to level the playing field. I was confident in my abilities, strengthened by Caelus' air powers, but why start the fight at a disadvantage?

"Excuse me," I said once I reached the counter. The elderly woman glanced up at me from her sudoku puzzle. "I'm looking for annatto seeds. Do you have any?"

"Don't get many people asking for those." The woman stood and rummaged in a fabric bin behind the counter. "Just one young woman lately, I think. There was a phase there for a while when everyone was taking them for the health benefits. Now they've moved on to kale or blueberries or whatever the new fad is. Ah, here we are." She held out a bag containing individually wrapped packages of annatto seeds. "You'll need a lemon to activate the full health benefits. Or was it a lime? I can't remember now."

I nodded briskly. "I'll take three packages. Oh, and any sage if you have it."

The woman rang up my purchases, and I left with a purposeful gait. By bedtime tonight, I hoped to make my first amulet.

CHAPTER VIII

The dishes had long since been cleared from the kitchen table, and Miranda and I bent over our work.

"How much sage do we need?" she murmured, her finger running down the recipe. "I don't know, this whole amulet-making thing feels hopeless. Why are we bothering?"

I ignored her—Miranda had been in a pessimistic mood ever since we went underground—and concentrated on grinding the annatto with a mortar and pestle I'd found in the back of a lower cupboard. Intention was as important as ingredients, if my experiments in my previous life were any indication, and I needed as much belief and power as I could muster to infuse into the annatto.

The front door slammed open, and footsteps pounded down the hall. Shu burst into the room, her eyes wild and tear tracks outlined by wet mascara dripping down her cheeks.

"Shu! What's wrong?" Miranda jumped up and ran to her sister.

I set my mortar down and studied Shu. My stomach clenched at the anticipation of bad news. Her chest heaved with emotion.

"Joy," she choked out. "They took Joy. I don't know where."

Miranda sank onto the nearest chair. Shu joined her at the table, her hands twisting in her lap.

"Why did they take her?" I asked softly. Joy's nerves this morning echoed through my memory, but I shut them down. Sending her to the order had been the right call at the time. Every move was a risk. My stomach still churned.

"They suspected her because Miranda drove her car to Agatha's house the other night." Shu sniffed loudly. "What are they going to do to her? Before yesterday, I wouldn't have been concerned. But they have the power to do whatever they want."

"And the motive," I said. "They want power and immortality, and they seemed determined to get it, no matter the cost." I sighed and laid my palms on the table. "You'll have to be careful, Shu. They have no reason to suspect you, so let's keep it that way."

"Maybe I shouldn't be here." Shu looked wildly around. Miranda clutched her hand as if terrified Shu would run away on the spot.

"None of us should." I stood. "Now that they know Joy was with us, this house is compromised. We need to move tonight."

"But where?" Miranda whispered.

I had no idea, but a leader didn't show doubts to her followers.

"Leave that to me. Pack your things, Miranda. Shu, can you drive us?"

Shu nodded mutely, and Miranda rushed upstairs. I followed more sedately, my mind whirling over this new development. Our small list of allies was down one, and our headquarters were useless. Where could we go to hide and still make a difference?

"Jerome," I said once I'd called him from the privacy of my bedroom. I threw clothes into my backpack while I talked. "Miranda and I can't stay in this house anymore. Do you have any ideas of where we could go? We're not picky."

"Right. The offer of my place is still open." When I grunted a negative—I didn't relish Miranda as a third wheel—Jerome paused a moment to think. "I have a buddy with a furnished shed at the back of his mechanic garage. It's out of the way and hard to see from the road. I can call him right now."

"Please."

I signed off and heaved a sigh. I was grateful to Jerome—he'd come up with a solution immediately, with no further questions asked—but the prospect of living in a shed didn't thrill me.

Still, it was better than whatever fate Joy was now experiencing. I shivered. Would Hazel and the others truly harm one of their own? Would they wipe Joy's memories or worse? I didn't know enough about Hazel to hazard a guess.

As soon as we set up headquarters in a new location, our next priority needed to be springing Joy from whatever holding cell she'd been stuffed into.

I marched downstairs with my backpack on my back. Miranda and Shu were waiting for me.

"Grab some groceries," I instructed. "Nothing that needs refrigeration. I have somewhere for us to stay."

Miranda and Shu scurried into the kitchen, eager for something to do in this crisis. When they returned with two grocery bags, I addressed Shu.

"You'll need to pretend you're still a loyal order member," I said to her. "If we want a snowball's chance in hell of freeing Joy, we need your intel. Hoodwink whoever is necessary, and don't visit our hideout unless you really need to."

Shu blanched but nodded. "I'll do what I can. The last thing I want is to pretend that this is all okay, but we need to get Joy back."

"That's right," I said, relieved that she hadn't put up a fight. I was hesitant sending her back into the lion's den, but we needed information. "Miranda and I will focus on deciphering the book and making amulets."

We followed Shu out the door and entered her small hatchback. After a few minutes of driving, I directed Shu to stop. Miranda gave Shu a hug which she returned, clinging to the other girl.

"Stay safe, Shu," Miranda whispered. "Call if you get into trouble."

Shu nodded. We hopped out a block from the address, and Shu pulled away. Miranda followed me in silence for a minute.

"Where are we going, anyway?" she asked, scuffing her feet on the sidewalk.

"Jerome has a friend with space for us behind his shop. He texted me the address. It will be rough, but it will keep us dry." I debated telling Miranda exactly how rough I was expecting, but I figured that was better experienced than described. "It will do for now."

Miranda trailed behind me as I strode forward, eager to put four walls between us and the outside world full of dangerous order members. For a moment, I reflected on the direction of my life. How long would this running and hiding go on for? We were very far from finding the Thorn, let alone recovering the Leaf and Seed. Now, Joy was captured, the others were in danger, and we couldn't show our faces on the streets. When would Hazel and the others stop hunting us?

When we either weren't a threat anymore, or we showed them we were too strong to mess with. I bared my teeth in a mirthless grin. I knew which one I preferred. First thing tomorrow, we would finish preparing an amulet. If Hazel wanted a fight, I would give one to her.

The mechanic shop was closed at this late hour, and few cars whizzed by us on the road. Miranda's uncertain glance touched on my face, but I didn't show my own hesitation.

"Around the back, he told me." I strode forward, along a chain-link fence that skirted the property. We dodged old tires and a rusted truck chassis on our way to the backyard. It was entirely paved, although weeds sprouted out of cracks in the asphalt.

A small outbuilding stood in the corner, half-hidden by an old Chevy van. Pallets leaned against the side, and a window was smeared with grime. I almost turned around to march over to Jerome's place, third wheel be damned, but I didn't want to put him in danger. This favor was enough. If Hazel found out that Jerome and I were involved, who knew how she might use that information?

"It looks dry," I said to a disbelieving Miranda. "Come on, let's see how we can get inside."

The door fit better than I'd expected, and inside was a pleasant surprise. Instead of a full garage of oily vehicle parts, a makeshift suite greeted my eyes. It was dusty, to be sure, but a ratty old couch stood across from a rickety table with a hot plate on it, a bed moldered in the corner, and a bathroom even graced the opposite wall. I sighed in relief, despite the musty smell.

"This will do," I said with more satisfaction than I truly felt. I wished my budget would allow for a hotel stay—it was what March would have done, no question—but Morgan didn't have extra money to throw around. "We'll kit it out better in the morning."

Miranda's lip trembled, but she didn't give way to her emotions. She nodded tightly and walked with stiff legs to the bathroom. When the door shut behind her, I flopped onto the couch and sneezed from the cloud of dust that enveloped me.

"Not on my watch," I muttered. I lifted my arms and pulled a few air threads. A wind tore through the shed, gathering dust in a choking storm. I held my sleeve over my face and ran to the door. Once it swung open, the air funneled through and took the dust with it.

When the shed was as clean as I could manage with air threads, I marched outside and performed my warding weave with the strands outside. When satisfied with my work, I returned to the couch and flopped onto it once more, unaccompanied by dust. I smiled and closed my eyes.

Caelus rose from my arm. "It could be worse," he said conversationally. "Hazel could be torturing you with amulets right now."

"Such a ray of sunshine," I said with my eyes closed. "Yes, it's bad, but it could be worse. And tomorrow, we'll make an amulet. It's about time something went our way."

Once Miranda exited the bathroom, calm but with red-rimmed eyes, I found some extra blankets in a chest. I waved her toward the bed and unfolded the blankets on the couch for myself. Night pressed down on me, relieved only by a faint glow of orange streetlights through the grimy window. It took a long time to fall asleep.

When I awoke the next morning, Caelus floated above my face, waiting for me to wake up.

"That's really creepy, you know that, right?" I grumbled at him quietly. I wriggled to an upright position, and he fell into place on my arm.

"Of course I know," he said. "Why else do you think I do it? Now that you're finally up, we need to talk."

I scrubbed my face with my hands, and Caelus bobbed around with the motion.

"Okay, talk," I said. "What about?"

"Things have gone from bad to worse. We have the Book, yes, but the order stole the artifacts and captured Joy, we're no closer to finding the Thorn, and we're hiding in a smelly hole."

"We're going to make some amulets today," I said in my defense. "It's not all bad news."

"Why don't you just steal some of the elders' amulets from that cabin in the orchard?"

"Because," I said with exaggerated patience. "They will have certainly moved them by now. We broke through their wards, so Hazel knows the amulets would never be safe from us there."

"In any case, amulets are a stop-gap measure," he said. "They will act as protection, but they're not a step forward. They won't get us further toward finding the Thorn or rescuing the other artifacts. Or Joy," he said as an afterthought.

I slumped against the couch. "You're right. We need to take drastic action if we want to get ahead. You should look for an elemental ally to help."

"What?" Caelus squeaked. "I didn't mean that."

"What else can we do? An elemental can at least find the artifacts, no? You could if you went there, but I know you don't want to risk it with your dormancy on the line. A quick question—a favor—wouldn't be that much to ask an ally, would it? Don't you have any friends or elementals who owe you?"

Caelus was silent for a long moment.

"Yes, I have allies in the other plane," he said finally. "But what if my unveiling gathers unwanted attention? I don't have enough artifacts gathered yet, I'm sure of it."

"Then you'd better be quick," I said with as much confidence as I could inject into my voice. "In and out, get what you need and then leave."

Caelus squared his shoulders. "Okay. I can do this. Let's go outside where there's a breeze."

I folded back my blankets, shrugged into my coat, and carefully opened the door without waking Miranda. The pre-dawn air was cold, and I tucked my hands in my pockets.

"Okay, it's all on you now," I said.

Caelus spread his arms wide and closed his eyes. I watched, fascinated, as his hands slowly unraveled and joined silvery strands that drifted through the air. It was a slow process, and I grew bored by the time his elbows vanished.

A mighty jolt of shock and fear threw my heart into overdrive. Caelus' arms reformed, and he shrank against me.

"Air is coming," he said in a harsh whisper. "My worst fear."

CHAPTER IX

My adrenaline spiked. Air was Caelus' leader, the head of his element, and the exact elemental we wanted to avoid. I opened my mouth to soothe Caelus.

A blast of arctic air hit me broadside, followed by a dull roar as if from a hurricane in the distance. Scrap paper swirled in the paved yard. From a twister of silver threads, a humanoid figure formed.

"I have been waiting for you," Air said in a voice that somehow reminded me of both whistling wind and the breath of a mouse. "What artifacts have you found?"

"I've destroyed an ancient neck cuff and a cup," Caelus said in a small voice.

"No others?" Air's voice grew more terrible than before. Caelus cowered against me.

"We had a Leaf and a Seed, but they were stolen from us. We're planning to get them back soon," Caelus said with more confidence than the plan warranted. However, I approved of overpromising to Air if it meant Caelus escaping dormancy.

"Forget any other artifacts," Air boomed. "Focus all your might on the Leaf, Seed, and Thorn. Nothing else matters. Do you understand?"

"Yes," Caelus said quickly. "Yes, they will be in my possession soon."

"Do not fail me," Air said.

The elemental's threads dissolved into the whirling twister then exploded. When I blinked my eyes, the strands calmly drifted in the morning breeze once more.

Caelus and I were silent for a long time.

"So, that was strange," I said at last. "What's so important about these three artifacts? Why the sudden change of heart?"

"I wonder if that wasn't Air's goal all along," Caelus said slowly. "Was collecting artifacts just a cover for getting these three without explaining anything to me? We know that this fifth elemental Spirit will be released when the three are combined. Why doesn't Air want Spirit around?"

"What does Air know about Spirit that the rest of the elementals don't?" I wrapped my coat tighter around me. "Air wasn't very forthcoming. After you aren't in danger of being sent to dormancy, I suggest you demand some answers."

Caelus shivered. "I don't want answers that badly. I'll never be safe from dormancy unless I am Air itself."

I texted our little team then retreated from the dawn chill into the musty shed. Miranda was tossing on the bed, but she sat up when I entered. She looked bleary-eyed at me.

"Now what do we do?" she asked in a hopeless voice. Clearly, she hadn't recovered from her doldrums of yesterday.

I clucked my tongue. "We have plenty to do. I've asked Amanda and Shu to come this morning so we can make a plan. Did you think we would leave Joy to rot in whatever holding cell the elders have her in?"

"No," she said listlessly.

I narrowed my eyes at her. Something wasn't right. Miranda should be galvanized by my words, not apathetic.

"That's why I've called the others. We'll brainstorm the best strategy, then I'll give everyone a task. We need Joy, the stolen artifacts, the Thorn, and new amulets. Also, food and a sleeping bag wouldn't go amiss. You won't be bored today."

Miranda dragged herself out of bed and dressed while I gathered our scant provisions into a makeshift breakfast. By the time I was brushing crumbs off the table into my hand for disposal, a voice called from outside hesitantly.

"Morgan? Miranda?"

Miranda slouched to the door and yanked it open. Shu and Amanda entered with hugs for their sister and wide eyes for our abode. Shu's lips thinned, and Amanda's jaw dropped open in horror.

"Are you sure you don't want to hide out at my apartment?" she said weakly. "We could be careful."

"We want to preserve your status as loyal order members for as long as possible," I said before Miranda could answer. I moved swiftly to the door to shut it. Movement caught my eye as a rust-colored pigeon waddled out of sight behind a tire. Had Beaky followed me here? I shut the door with a suppressed smile and turned to the others. "They'll be watching you closely after the debacle with Joy. I hope you were both careful about being followed." They both nodded mutely. "Us staying with you would put you in danger, both of being captured and of us losing a source of information. It's rough here, for certain, but we'll clean it up today. No one from the order would think of looking for us here."

"That's for sure," Shu muttered.

"Come in and have a seat," I instructed. My hand waved at the couch. The others traipsed to the furniture while I pulled up a rickety kitchen chair and sat in front of the three. "We have lots to do. Our priority is Joy. What do we know?"

"I heard that Hazel searched Joy's grandparents' house," Shu said. "My mother told me. I don't know whether it was a wild guess of Hazel's because they're Joy's family, or…"

"Or they're getting information out of Joy," I finished for the reluctant Shu.

Miranda and Amanda glanced at each other with identical expressions of fear.

"They wouldn't torture her, would they?" Miranda whispered.

"They have plenty of amulets that would force her to say things without pain," Amanda said, but she looked worried.

"They're not going to keep her in a hotel room," I said. "Let's think of where she might be."

"Agatha's house at the orchard," said Amanda.

"Hazel's place, or Beatrice's," said Shu.

I snapped my fingers. "Good. We'll check every location. Start with the ones in town. Amanda, choose two to check this morning. You need to go to work after to avoid suspicion."

"I can call in sick," Shu said quickly. Her knee jiggled. "We need to find Joy."

"Rosemary will have to run the salon alone," Miranda said. She picked at her fingernails. "She'll be the only one there, what with Joy and me missing. That will be even more suspicious."

"Does Rosemary suspect that we're up to something?" I asked. "She was so keen to take down the order before."

The others glanced at each other.

"She's not quite herself," Amanda said finally. "Still."

"She's nuts," Shu said flatly. She jumped up, unable to keep still. "I don't trust her to keep her trap shut. She might be calm now, but that loose cannon could blow at any time. She's not someone I want keeping my secrets. There's paranoia, and there's Rosemary. I vote for keeping her in the dark."

I sighed. Our list of allies was not a long one. "I'm already leaving her out of the loop, so I'll continue to do so. I agree, our situation is too precarious to confide in someone we don't trust. Okay, Shu, you check out the other location. Whatever you two do, don't try to rescue Joy on your own." I looked at them both sternly. "Find out where they're keeping her and report back. We'll make a proper plan. Miranda and I will make an amulet today that we can use for our rescue mission."

"But what if she's hurt or alone?" Shu paced the open space in front of the door. "I'm not leaving her there if she's hurt and I have a chance to rescue her."

"Don't do anything on your own, do you hear?" I stared at Shu, who glared back defiantly. Finally, her eyes dropped in submission.

"Fine," she grumbled, back to pacing. "But we'd better have a quick turnaround."

"We will," I said, relieved that Shu had backed down. The others were willing to follow my lead, but Shu was more headstrong. It was one more reason to keep a firm tether on all of them. If Shu rushed headlong into danger without thinking, we would likely be down two team members instead of saving one.

"Okay, you have your marching orders," I said to them. "Off you go." Once they stood and Amanda and Shu moved to the door, I stopped them with a hand. Shu jiggled in place. "Wait. Don't forget to keep asking about the Leaf and Seed. Amanda, see what you can get out of Denise. Shu, whoever you can contact."

They nodded and left. Miranda looked at me with uncertainty.

"What should I do?"

"Today," I said with satisfaction, "we are going to make an amulet."

Miranda and I cleared the table and set up our supplies. A small cage with a fat hamster in the middle was in pride of place, bought by Miranda this morning from a nearby pet shop. Surrounding the cage, I sprinkled raw sunflower and pumpkin seeds, which the hamster eyed greedily. Miranda dusted the seeds with flakes of hot chili peppers then looked at the instruction page with a skeptical eye.

"This recipe is super weird," she said. "I feel like I'm baking the grossest cake ever."

"It's very strange," I agreed. "But the elders have been using these recipes to make amulets for years. Don't forget to light the candles."

Miranda sighed heavily. She scraped a matchhead against its box and held it to one of three pillar candles in a triangle around the cage. The hamster watched her movements, its nose twitching. I laid a fork on the table before me that I'd commandeered from the kitchenette.

"Okay, I think we're ready." I stared at the hamster, who showed no signs of wanting to use its exercise wheel. "I knew we should have bought a gerbil instead. Or a rat. They love to exercise."

"But this one is so cute." Miranda bent over and cooed at the rodent. "Hi there, Hamantha. Do you want to go for a little run?"

I rolled my eyes when Miranda wasn't looking and placed my hands on the table for support. "If you get the hamster moving, I'll perform the ritual."

Caelus bloomed from my arm and looked over our handiwork without comment. I took that as approval and closed my eyes. The hum bursting from my throat was reedy and high-pitched.

"Lower," Caelus instructed. "I'll tell you when the threads do something interesting."

"Hamantha is on her wheel," Miranda said.

I peeked from under my eyelids. From her position draped over the edge of the table, Miranda limply held a pumpkin seed through the cage next to the hamster's wheel. It was running hard to reach the seed, and loose pieces of thread drifted off the animal with its movement. Those were the bits I wanted to capture to complete the spell.

I lowered my hum's pitch and poured my intention into my spell. I wanted this fork as an amulet to promote clear thinking, and since intention was half of amulet making, I directed my thoughts in an intense stream toward the fork.

Slowly, threads from the seeds, chili pepper, candles, and hamster drifted toward the fork. They wrapped around the piece of cutlery with languid movements. When the migration slowed, I cut off my hum and fully opened my eyes.

"Well, something happened," Caelus said without enthusiasm.

"What were you expecting, fireworks?" I picked up the fork and examined its threads.

"Did it work?" Miranda said once I'd stopped humming.

Caelus tsked. "Not nearly as strong as ones made by the order. It looks more like the weak ones from your old group, Morgan."

I glared at Caelus—mainly because I didn't want Miranda to know about my past life, but also because Caelus was insulting me as usual, and a glare was a fitting punishment—but he was right. The threads surrounding the fork were paltry, a mere fraction of the simplest amulet that the sisters used.

"What did I do wrong?" I pulled the translated page of the Book of Souls closer and ran my fingers down the words. "Are you sure you translated this correctly, Miranda?"

"Pretty sure," she said with a defensive shrug. "I'm not exactly a medieval scholar, but I know my way around a Latin dictionary."

"Sorry, I didn't mean it like that. I just don't know what went wrong." I sat back, unsure what to do next but unwilling to let Miranda see my uncertainty. "I'll study this a bit more, see if I can figure out what happened. How about you get us some groceries at the corner store, stretch your legs a bit?"

Miranda pushed herself up, clearly relieved to escape our smelly shed and our fruitless task despite her lethargy. When she was gone, I read over the instructions more carefully, but nothing struck me as wrong.

"Were my intentions not strong enough?" I wondered aloud.

Caelus crossed his arms. "Maybe. Or maybe you need more experience. There's probably a reason these things aren't just lying around everywhere. The sisters don't know how to make them, and neither do the mothers. It must be a secret skill carefully taught to new elders and honed over years." Caelus shrugged. "Or they have a secret sauce that the book doesn't mention."

A knock cut through the sound of drills and compressors from the mechanic shop outside. With a creak, the door swung open, and Jerome's head peeked inside. His face relaxed in relief when he saw I was alone, but a frown deepened on his forehead at the interior of the shed.

"This place is a dump," he said after he'd shut the door behind him. "I'm sorry I mentioned it to you. Are you sure you don't want to stay at my place?"

"It's fine. I don't want the elders to know about you." I stood and walked over to him, happy for the distraction from my amulet failure. "It's safest for everyone if I'm here."

Jerome ground his teeth in frustration, but he didn't deny it, which surprised me. I would have expected him to protest. When he glanced at the door, my suspicions about his secrets returned anew.

I stepped closer to Jerome, not wanting to waste an opportunity and more than willing for a distraction from my terrible surroundings and difficult tasks. My life was closing in on me—friends disappearing, artifacts gone, home uninhabitable—but Jerome was still here.

My hands rested on Jerome's shoulders then traveled over his coat collar to touch his bare neck. Our eyes met, and the heat of desire flared in his gaze. My lips opened, and Jerome's hands on my hips drew my body closer to his. Our fronts met, and the warmth of his body dialed my attraction up to eleven.

I wanted him, and I wanted him now. In a frenzy, I tugged off my long-sleeved shirt and pulled it over my head. Jerome groaned and ran his hands over my naked stomach, now covered in goosebumps from the chill of the shed. He leaned down and kissed my hand, my wrist, my forearm, clearly intending to bring his lips all the way up. I wasn't about to stop him.

He paused. "Morgan," he said huskily. "What are these?"

CHAPTER X

I glanced down to see what had arrested his delicious movements. His fingers traced the white scars that crisscrossed my inner forearms. Fiorella, the woman who had inhabited this body before me, must have suffered from mental health issues that had resulted in her cutting herself.

The scars were a physical reminder of the secret I still hadn't shared with Jerome. If I told him everything, would he reciprocate? I was tired of hiding from him, and tired of trying to understand his secrets and why he was so tense lately.

I bent down and retrieved my shirt. My body screamed for me to continue our activities, but my mind had other plans.

"Sit down," I said. "I have something to tell you."

Jerome walked over to the couch and sat on the edge gingerly. His eyes raked my face, searching for the answers I was about to give him.

"Is everything okay?" He took my hand in his, and I savored the feeling of being enveloped by his large, warm grasp.

"I'm fine now," I said. "But I haven't told you everything about me, and I think it's time. You know about Caelus and my abilities with air. You know about, well, magic, for lack of a better word."

Jerome nodded but didn't speak, for which I was grateful. Finding the right words was more difficult that I'd imagined.

"You remember how I explained that everyone has their own color threads," I started. "They represent their soul, if you will. Well, a few months ago, my body died. But, because of an amulet's help, my threads transferred to a new body." I waved at my figure. "This one. I've only occupied it for a few months. The previous inhabitant left when the body died—from its own causes, nothing I did, by the way—but Caelus brought it back to life, intending to use it for himself. My intrusion was an accident."

Jerome's brow furrowed so deeply I wondered if he would ever be able to smile again.

"You're saying that you used to be someone different."

"My mind is what it has always been," I corrected him. "But my body was different, yes. These scars?" I held up my arms. "They were not caused by me."

"So, who were you before?" Jerome's body was tense like he planned to leap off the couch at any moment. I didn't blame him—there was a reason I hadn't told him before now—but I hoped he would stick around until his questions were answered.

"My name used to be March Feynman. I was a fifty-five-year-old businesswoman in Vancouver. I'd followed some unfortunate paths near the end and made mistakes I wish I hadn't, which resulted in my death." I twisted my mouth wryly. "But then I wouldn't be where I am now, so it all worked out."

"You're fifty-five," he repeated.

I wrinkled my nose. I'd known that would be a sticking point. "Yes."

"Okay." Jerome stood and put his hands behind his head. He didn't look at me. "Right. Okay. I need some time to think about that." He stepped away then turned back to me. "Are you going to be okay here?"

Amid the turmoil I knew Jerome was going through, he'd remembered my well-being. I smiled warmly.

"I'll be fine. Go. I'll text you if anything changes."

Jerome strode out of the shed without glancing back. I leaned against the couch, drained by my revelations. A large part of me was convinced that I'd ruined everything. Would he ever want to see me again?

But a relationship built on lies would eventually crumble. I didn't regret telling Jerome my biggest secret, but if our burgeoning relationship was over, by my hand, I would mourn it deeply.

Miranda was fetching food, and the others were gathering intel. I wanted to take another crack at making an amulet, but before I could move to the table where my ingredients were laid out, Caelus blossomed out of my arm.

"You told Jerome about your body-switching antics." His eyebrows almost disappeared into his thready hair. "I didn't think that was ever going to happen. Too bad he left you over it."

"He didn't leave me. He just needs time to think about it." I wasn't at all certain of this fact but needed to say it out loud to convince myself. I pushed down the last of my unslaked ardor and walked to the table, Caelus trailing in the air behind me. "Now I have time to work on the amulet."

"Is that really our priority? You tried the amulet, it didn't work. Don't bang your head against that wall when you have a Thorn to find. Or did you forget our ultimate mission? I know there's a lot going on, but still. Focus on the artifacts."

"Right." I scrubbed my face then picked up the Book of Souls. Miranda's translations were next, along with her Latin dictionary. "Miranda's done a lot of the Book, but there are some pages still undeciphered. Maybe I can take a stab at them, see if there are any further clues."

"It won't be anything the elders don't know, but at least we'll be on equal footing with them." Caelus rested insubstantial fingers on the Book in my hands. "Let's try."

I flopped onto the threadbare couch and cracked open the Book. My fingers flipped through pages I recognized until the last third, the elders-only section. Miranda had translated the first few pages of solid writing, and the next several dozen were clearly amulet instructions. At the back, two pages of text greeted my eyes.

"This might take a while," I warned Caelus. "I have a smattering of Latin, helpful for grammar, mainly, but I'm going to have to look up most words in the dictionary."

"You'd better get going, then." Caelus settled against my arm and gazed at the Book expectantly. I sighed and looked up the first word in the dictionary.

An hour later, I'd deciphered the first half page, and my eyes were dry from staring at the foreign words. I held my translated scribbles aloft to read in its entirety for the first time.

The believers traveled across the ocean in search of a place to keep the Thorn safe. Because of its great power and importance to the goddess, the believers were willing to lay down their lives to protect it. For they knew that when the goddess returned to this world, she would gather her faithful and they would be exalted. For all people join the goddess after death, and when released from her prison, the goddess will reshape the Earth with fire and water to house her faithful, whether living or dead. The Great Flood was the last time the goddess was allowed to reign freely and impose her will on those who did not follow her.

The believers traveled to the far west in search of a safe abode for the precious Thorn.

"That's not helpful at all," Caelus said when I'd finished reading out loud. "'Reshape the Earth'. What is that supposed to mean?"

"I'm not sure." I drummed my fingers on the table. "It's repeating the apocalyptic warning that we read earlier, though. The Great Flood—that sounds an awful lot like Noah and the ark from the Bible. A massive flood is documented in the earliest records of civilization from numerous sources. Do you think it was caused by the Spirit elemental?"

"Maybe." Caelus frowned. "That sounds like a huge imbalance in the elements. No wonder she was locked away. And there's nothing in the Book so far about where they actually put the Thorn. The far west, that's it. So, hopefully somewhere nearby."

"Hopefully." I leaned back against the couch, drained from my efforts and disappointed that they hadn't been more fruitful. "But if we don't know where the Thorn is, hopefully neither does Hazel."

Miranda arrived shortly after bearing grocery bags and wearing sunglasses and her hood. I pounced on the bags and assembled a late breakfast of eggs and toast, which we ate eagerly. I flipped through the amulet instructions while we ate.

"Miranda," I said eventually. "I'd like to try making an amulet that gives the bearer a burst of speed. We couldn't get the other amulet to work, but maybe it was too complex to start out with. This one is far simpler."

"Worth a try," she said, doubt coloring her tone.

"I'll get the sassafras we need after breakfast." I slammed the Book shut with decision. "There's that specialty grocer on Cormorant Drive. It's a bit of a walk, but the fresh air will be nice. You can finish translating the last few pages. I got a start, here." I pushed my page of notes toward her, along with the Book. "So, start from where I left off."

Miranda took the offered page without enthusiasm, then she frowned. "I don't think you should go wandering on Cormorant Drive, not with Hazel and the order looking for you. They know that's our usual neighborhood. Maybe I should come with you." She didn't look enthused at the prospect and glanced longingly at her bed. "More eyes on the lookout."

"I'll be fine." I quelled Miranda's concern with an airy wave of my hand. "Caelus is with me. He'll keep an eye out."

"Still." Miranda put her hands on her hips, ready to press her point. "More is better. Trust me to have your back. I can stand guard at the shop entrance while you buy stuff."

"It would be far more useful to our side if you translated this morning." I pushed the Book closer to her. "Thanks for thinking of me, but let's divide and conquer."

I left a disgruntled Miranda in the kitchen and prepared myself to leave our sanctuary in the entry hall. On went sunglasses and back went my hair into a ponytail, subsequently covered by my hood. I couldn't do much more than that. Caelus could keep a watchful eye on our surroundings. I gathered notes for one of my clients—might as well not waste the opportunity to leave this place—and sailed out the door.

The fresh breeze of a mid-morning spring day was balm to my psyche. I inhaled deeply, relieved to be rid of the moldy smell of the shed, even if the air smelled faintly of tires and oil from the mechanic shop. I slunk around the side, but no one spotted me, and I joined the sidewalk without detection.

I stopped at the specialty grocery store for sassafras first, pretending I was making homemade root beer. It took me whole minutes to extract myself from conversation with the sudoku-playing proprietor, who grew overly enthusiastic at my pretended soda aspirations. Next, I dropped off my recent notes for the toy store, apologizing for my handwritten pages and citing a printer breakdown. I didn't own a printer, but I hadn't thought it wise to add another stop at a copy center to pick up my pages. Caelus perched on my shoulder and peered at our surrounds the entire time.

After my successful stops, I walked on a road parallel to Cormorant Drive to avoid onlookers. When I passed Eleventh Avenue, I paused. Upper Crust, the bakery Jerome worked at, was one block away. My stomach growled. I hadn't eaten a lemon tart for days, which my body reminded me was entirely unacceptable.

But Jerome was in there. I checked my watch. It wouldn't be long before his break. If I were patient, I could sneak in while he was out and fetch my tarts without him seeing me. The last thing I wanted to do was to put pressure on Jerome. He needed to process my massive revelation, and me turning up at his work wouldn't help that. I wished I could see him, touch him, kiss him, but I knew he wouldn't thank me for that.

I loitered at the corner with my hood up for fifteen minutes, then I peeked in the window. The kitchen area was occupied only by a sandwich cook and two servers. I gave a sigh of relief that nevertheless twisted my heart.

Kaylee smiled when I approached the front counter. "Hi, Morgan. I haven't seen you for a while. Three tarts as usual?"

"You know it," I said, taking off my sunglasses to speak with her.

"You just missed Jerome." She slid three tarts into a paper bag and passed it to me. "He should be back soon if you want to wait. He's in a bit of a mood, could probably use cheering up."

"No, that's fine, thanks," I said quickly, handing her my money. "I'll catch up with him later."

I retreated before Kaylee's confused look resulted in further questions. She was probably putting two and two together and wondering if I had something to do with Jerome's mood. Just because she was right didn't mean I wanted to talk about it with her.

I munched thoughtfully on my first tart, my sunglasses firmly in place on my face once more. How long would Jerome ponder the intricacies of my identity? Would we be able to get past this, or had I ruined our relationship forever?

"You think too much," Caelus said. "And very loudly. Jerome will figure it out. What's a little body-switching? He managed to wrap his head around my existence, after all."

"Only just," I said. "He still isn't comfortable with you, that's for sure. Well, there's nothing I can do about it now. The cat's out of the bag, and that's that."

My feet took me down the next road. I passed the alley, and all of Caelus' threads jolted.

"Morgan," he gasped. "Watch out!"

CHAPTER XI

An arcing ray of threads shot toward me out of the alley like a lightning bolt. I dived to the side to avoid it, but I was too slow. The strands surrounded me and intertwined with my own. Caelus froze beside me, his expression caught in a rictus of horror. I landed on the ground with a thump, but I couldn't make a move to catch myself. I was paralyzed.

"Finally," Hazel's voice drifted toward me. She walked into view, and I had a clear sight of her sensible footwear in a flashy shade of apple-red. "You've been hiding—quite cleverly, I might add—but you left your hidey-hole, and that was your mistake. I've had people watching out for you."

She touched her bracelet and muttered a word. The strands slithered off my legs, and I could move them again. Hazel hauled at my arm until I was upright. I wasted no time kicking her as hard as I could. All I received for my efforts was a hurt toe and Hazel's satisfied expression.

"You really have no idea who you're dealing with, do you?" she said. "Come along. We have things to talk about, you and I."

She yanked at my arm, and I stumbled along behind her. Parked in the alley behind Upper Crust was Hazel's sedan. Hazel opened the back door, forced my unresponsive torso inside, and slammed it shut. She climbed into the front seat and drove sedately onto the main road.

"Oh," Hazel said after a minute. "I suppose you'd like to talk, wouldn't you? I'm quite curious about you, Morgan Feynman. So, here."

She touched her bracelet and whispered a word. My face released from its frozen expression, and I wiggled my eyebrows and mouth in relief.

"What the hell did you do?" I spat out. "Where are you taking me?"

"Somewhere a little more private." Hazel turned right. "We have things to do that I don't want others to see."

"How did you find me?"

"Joy has been most forthcoming." Hazel glanced in the rearview mirror. "After enough encouragement. Although she's a terrible order member, she's a loyal friend, I'll give her credit for that. After my amulets didn't work, I had to resort to cruder methods of persuasion."

"What did you do to her?" I gasped. "Is she okay?"

"I suppose that depends on your definition of 'okay'. She's alive if that's what you mean." I gaped at the back of Hazel's head, and she clucked her tongue at me. "You are a thorn in my side, Morgan. Thorn," she said with a chuckle. "Excuse the pun. It was a lot of work getting information out of Joy, but it was worth it. Because while she spilled the beans about your likely whereabouts, she also let slip about your continued possession."

Caelus stiffened next to me but wisely kept silent. I rearranged my face into a frown of confusion while I got to work on the paralysis magic. It was sticky, to be sure, but if I could throw off Thea's mind-control amulet, surely I could eventually wear away this one.

"I don't know what you mean."

"Oh, come now." Hazel glanced at me again in the mirror. "Don't be coy. Joy mentioned speaking to your spirit, so I know he still possesses you. Clearly, the exorcism didn't work. But Joy also described your wind powers, and only a fool wouldn't have recognized what they signified." She gave a long-suffering sigh. "The rest of the order are fools."

The memory of Starr—a previous sister hellbent on destroying the order—realizing that I was possessed crossed my mind, but I kept my mouth shut. I didn't know what Starr was up to, but I didn't want to put her on Hazel's radar, especially when it turned out she'd been right about the order's terrible goals.

"What does it matter to you about what my powers do?" I said slowly. My mind churned between Hazel's motives and her paralysis magic. What was Hazel's game?

"I've been coming at this the wrong way," Hazel said. She flipped her turn signal on and changed lanes, heading north to the water's edge. "I thought eliminating your threat was the most sensible path. But an elemental in your body is a gift to be used, not thrown aside."

"And how are you going to use him?" I shared a glance with Caelus.

"I've been waiting a long time to release Spirit," Hazel said in a thoughtful tone. "Longer than you can imagine. The order credits Agatha for finding the Leaf, but she never would have done it without my guidance. She is revered as the leader of the order, but I'm the real driver. Everyone does my bidding through Agatha, my idealistic, naïve, vapid mouthpiece."

"What's your game?" I said. "Why do you want Spirit released? Is it for immortality and power, like the Book of Souls says?"

Hazel barked out a laugh. "I'm already immortal, or close enough. Millennia I've been waiting to collect all three artifacts together." She held up her left hand, whose ring finger wore a plain gold band surrounded by threads. "Spirit gave me the power to live forever. I was there when she was locked away. We have a special connection." Hazel gazed at the ring for a moment before returning her attention to the road.

I looked at Caelus. *Do elementals get married?* I asked him. *Because that's what a ring like that usually means to humans.*

No, he replied. *Allies, not friends or lovers or any other of the endless permutations of relations you humans have. But I don't know what this Spirit elemental is. Maybe she's a whole new type with new rules. By the way, Hazel has the Leaf and Seed in that locket around her neck.*

I glanced at Hazel's necklace, which sported a large locket with threads leaking from it.

"So, you want to bring back Spirit because you and she are close," I said in summation. The paralysis magic started to fray, and I pushed my will into it with renewed vigor. "Fine. You have the Leaf and Seed, and everything you need to find the Thorn. What do you want me for?"

"Your body," she said eagerly.

"That's a bold statement, considering we just met," I said with a barely repressed smile. "You're a forward one, aren't you?"

"Not like that," Hazel said, her smug façade cracking for the first time with irritation. "I don't want to—no, I need to switch bodies soon. How do you think immortality works? I transfer my essence to a new host when my current body grows too old. This one has a few more useful years in it, but how can I pass up such a perfect vessel like you?"

A shiver ran down my back. Hazel had switched forms like I had, but for thousands of years. I had no doubt that she could take over my body with ease. Just like I'd managed to subdue Caelus when I'd first arrived in this body, so too would such an experienced soul have no trouble pushing me down. Just seeing how my amulet creation compared to the strength of the order's amulets told me that I was outmatched.

"Your body is perfect." Hazel turned down a leafy street with an empty playing field at the end. When she parked, houses were hidden from view by large hedges. We were effectively alone. She unbuckled and twisted to look at me fully. "It's young, contains a captive air elemental, and it's trusted by your rogue members. I can mine whatever information your motley group has gathered, then go back to Beatrice and continue our great work to release Spirit."

"My air elemental isn't captive," I said. With a few more pushes of my will, the magic holding me down would disintegrate. "We are a partnership."

"That's your arrangement. Controlling an elemental will give me an advantage, and any advantage I can get is helpful finding the Thorn. I have loftier goals than the other order members. Spirit and I are meant to be together. We were together, once, before our sundering. When she was captured, my world fell apart, even though I knew it was coming. Spirit has promised me that once she is released, she will gather me into her essence, and we will be together forever."

I stared at Hazel, whose face had grown ecstatic at her hoped-for future, her eyes closed above a beatific smile.

Is she for real? Caelus muttered in my head.

I nodded faintly, my eyes not leaving Hazel's face. The time for talking was almost over. What else was there to say when one's opponent veered into madness? Blending essences with her millennia-gone elemental lover seemed a far-fetched ideal, but so too did her body-jumping antics, and I knew how possible that was. Hazel had a lot of skin in this game, and she was about to take mine.

I broke the final thread holding me down, then I glanced at Caelus. *Are you ready to fight?*

Quicker than a whip, Hazel's hand thrust through the gap between the front seats and grabbed the lapel of my coat in bony fingers that had far greater strength than expected. She wrenched me forward, and I flew against the front passenger seat.

I flailed at her hand with my newly mobile arms, scratching and pulling, but I might as well have been clawing at a rock for all the reaction I got. I raised my hand to poke at her eyes— a handy self-defense trick I'd learned from Shu—but Hazel's other hand slammed into my forehead. Something metal pressed into my skin.

My limbs stopped working again. Threads burst forth from the metal amulet between my forehead and Hazel's hand. With dizzying speed, they looped around my body and hers, pulling Hazel's green and purple threads along her arm and toward my body. Hazel was transferring her essence right now.

CHAPTER XII

Caelus! I shrieked in my head. *Help me push her back.*

Caelus' silver strands flooded up our body and surrounded our head in a dense cloud of threads. I watched in horror as Hazel's strands pushed against Caelus'.

What could I do? My own burgundy threads caught my eye. Could I do the same as Caelus and use my strands to push against the intruder? I concentrated—half of thread manipulation was in the intent—but my threads didn't budge. I wasn't an elemental, and I didn't have an amulet like Hazel did.

But I did have a body, and I was still in control of it.

I brought my hand up. With a motion like a darting snake, I rammed my outstretched fingers into Hazel's closed eyes.

Hazel recoiled with a cry of pain. She clutched her hand to her face, and my contact with the amulet ceased. All her green and purple threads slithered away from me.

I didn't waste time. My hand tore the golden locket from around her neck. I fumbled at the sedan's door handle, leaping onto the sidewalk and sprinting away across the muddy field until I lost the sedan from sight down a road on the other side of the park. My feet pounded the pavement. For good measure, I sent a blast of air behind me just in case Hazel was in pursuit. After a minute of dodging through alleys and around parked vehicles, I flung myself inside a dense laurel hedge and panted furiously.

Caelus blossomed out of my arm. "That was too close. She almost had us. She didn't anticipate my superior thread abilities—"

"Or my self-defense skills," I said. "She almost had us before that."

"But we're not possessed. And, bonus, we have the Leaf and Seed back."

I held up the locket so we could both admire it, then I tucked it into my pocket for safekeeping. When I could think more clearly, Miranda's face popped into my mind's eye. She had warned me about the dangers of wandering Cormorant Drive alone. She had even offered to watch my back. I'd dismissed her. I always considered myself the most competent person in the room—usually it was true—but had I been hampering our team's efforts with my desire to do everything my way? Miranda had been right, and it was only by the skin of my teeth that I'd escaped Hazel and not jeopardized the entire mission. I vowed to consider the others' opinions from now on before making my decisions.

"Look," I said, my heartbeat finally calming from thunder to the patter of elephant feet. "Now we know our focus is to get those three artifacts. Not that we didn't know that before, but—" I swallowed. "It's more important than ever. With the motivation of obsessive love, Hazel will stop at nothing to release her former lover. From what she's said so far, I doubt she has any concerns about the state of the world once Spirit is out."

"Is that what she was going on about?" Caelus stared at me. "I was trying to figure out what she meant by 'connection' and all that. You think this Spirit elemental came to the physical world and possessed a human?"

"And Hazel, or whatever name she used to go by, fell in love with her." I raised my eyebrow at Caelus. "Do you think it's possible that Spirit loved her too, despite being an elemental?"

Caelus shrugged, although his eyes were thoughtful. "Maybe. Especially if she had a human body that was prone to human emotions and hormones. I'm rather fond of you, despite your many faults. I could envision another elemental succumbing to that sort of nonsense."

"I love you too, Caelus." At Caelus' huff, I chuckled. "Okay, we know that Hazel will do whatever it takes to join

Spirit again, but whether Spirit feels the same or is just using Hazel for her freedom remains to be seen. It doesn't matter, at the end of the day. We can't let it get that far."

"This secret history," Caelus muttered. "How do I know nothing about it? Not a hint about a fifth element. I mean, I knew that the threads of living things were different, but I had no idea that they might function similarly to other elements or be unified by an elemental leader." He leaned against the wall next to me. "I was pretty high up in the chain of command, too. If Air was hiding this from me, what else is hidden? We only have Air's word that Spirit must be stopped."

I hauled myself to my feet and dusted off my bottom. We couldn't stay here forever, with Hazel roaming the streets. We would have to make a run for the relative safety of the shed and hope Hazel didn't spot us.

"We know that we need to get the artifacts back," I said. "Don't get sidetracked by unanswerable questions."

"Knowing the why will help us with the how and what," Caelus argued. "Why was Spirit locked up in the first place? We know nothing. How can I trust what Air tells me?"

I sighed in frustration. Caelus brought up interesting questions, but they were moot until we held all three artifacts in our hands. We needed to focus on the problems that we could solve right now.

"It doesn't matter," I said. "Besides, did you forget about the flood mentioned in the Book? Get on your game, Caelus, and help me figure out a way to get the Thorn."

Caelus' expression was thunderous, but I didn't see it for long. He melted into my arm, and his threads coiled into a dense ball of silver at my stomach. Discontent radiated from it.

"Fine," I said aloud. "I'll do it myself."

I peered out of the hedge. When the coast was clear—only one white minivan trundling past—I slid out of my hiding spot and joined the sidewalk.

"Keep an eye out behind us," I muttered to Caelus.

His threads remained stubbornly at my stomach. I rolled my eyes then scanned the road. Caelus was sulking, but that didn't help us evade Hazel. I brought my hands up to capture air between my fingers, hoping for a signal of approaching vehicles, but the threads slipped through. I frowned. Had Caelus removed my ability to use his air powers out of spite?

I sighed again. No, not spite. Caelus was reacting to my curt words. If I didn't want to end up like Hazel, I needed to listen to others around me. I was good at taking charge—too good, maybe—and it was difficult to let go of that control.

Plus, I could really use my powers back.

"Caelus," I said softly. "Come out. I'm sorry I ignored your concerns. Tell me what you're thinking."

I walked quietly for a long minute, giving Caelus time to consider. Finally, threads uncoiled, and silver flowed into my arm until Caelus' head and torso formed before me.

"You should be sorry," he said. "I have good questions."

"You do," I agreed. "What do you think we should do about our uncertainty of Air's motivations?"

Caelus' face relaxed now that I wasn't dismissing him. I pushed down my impatience while he thought.

"Of course, we need to get our hands on the artifacts," he said at last. "But I don't think we should destroy them until we know more. Air hasn't told me anything, and we can't take the Book of Souls at face value. We need more information before we destroy artifacts of such power."

"Okay," I said. Caelus peered at me, and I stared back. "That sounds reasonable. What, did you expect me to shut you down again?"

"Something like that."

"You have valid points, and I need to listen to good advice when I'm making decisions." I turned the corner on to the mechanic's road. "I need to try, at least."

"Wow." Caelus stuck his face into mine and looked at me

closely. "Are you feeling okay? Normally you're far more…"

"Direct?" I suggested. "Assertive?"

"Overbearing. Stubborn. Akin to a steamroller. But sure, assertive is a good euphemism."

I returned to the shed without mishap, skirting the tires and pallets with a familiar step. Maybe Caelus was right. Was I too overbearing? Did the others chafe under my leadership? I wouldn't mind—a leader couldn't be unduly swayed by public opinion, not if she wanted to get things done—except that my choices had led us nowhere. I might have the Leaf and Seed, but we were no closer to finding the Thorn, Joy was still in the Elders' clutches, and I couldn't make an amulet worthy of the name. Maybe it was time to listen to the others' ideas. They couldn't possibly bear fewer fruit than mine did.

Miranda was out, so I texted everyone and asked them to come to the shed when they could. They needed to know that Hazel was onto me. I didn't want any other sisters joining Joy in her prison.

Miranda arrived back a few minutes before noon, carrying two boxes of pizza. The hot tomato smell made my stomach growl indecently.

"Amanda can't make it, but Shu is coming in a minute." Miranda dropped the boxes on the table and sank into a chair with a sigh. "She said she has a surprise for us."

"I'm not a big fan of surprises today," I muttered, but Miranda didn't hear me. That was fine. I didn't want to explain Hazel's actions more than once.

When the door creaked open, I sat up straight. Shu entered looking tired and wan but oddly buzzing with energy. Behind her was someone new.

"Be ready," Caelus said. He must have spoken for my ears alone because Miranda didn't react to his words. She did, however, jump at the sight of the new woman.

"What are you doing?" Miranda gaped at Shu. "I thought you were on our side. How could you? You've ruined everything."

Shu held up her hand, her look pleading. "I promise, she's okay. We had a big talk last night. She's on our side." Shu tugged at the woman's hand, and I marveled at their similarities. The woman could be Shu, in twenty years' time, with the same straight black hair and warm skin. Shu looked at me. "Morgan, this is my mother, Lin. She's also a mother in the order."

"Pleased to meet you," Lin said in a crisp, clear voice. She smiled apologetically. "I understand this is a shock to you both, but I assure you, I mean you no harm. I'm here to help. For the past few years, I've been less than content with the order's missive. I haven't said anything until now, but I felt the urge last night when Shu visited. To my surprise, she told me that I was not alone in my misgivings."

Shu gave an encouraging nod when Lin glanced at her daughter.

"She could help a lot," Shu said eagerly. Her hands trembled at her sides. "Since she's a trusted mother of the order."

I glanced at Miranda, whose hesitant gaze gave me no answers, and then at Caelus.

What do you think? I said to him loudly in my head. *I'm not the trusting sort, but if she's being truthful, we could really use her.*

Hazel might have sent her, Caelus mused. *But her threads say she's telling the truth. I don't see any amulets on her, either, which means she's not hiding her threads' reaction through magical means. I'm inclined to believe her.*

Me too, I said. *Honestly, it's not much of a stretch. The order's missive is bizarre, and I'm only surprised that this is the first time anyone has rebelled.* "Okay," I said aloud.

"Welcome to the resistance, Lin. We could use your help."

Shu smiled in relief, and Lin nodded her head in acknowledgement. Miranda still looked unsure but willing to defer to my judgement. I frowned at Shu, whose shoulders were now trembling.

"Are you okay, Shu?" I asked. "Maybe you should sit down."

"No, I'm fine." Shu started to pace. "I can't keep still. It's like I've drunk a vat of coffee. There's no way I can sit."

"What happened?" Lin gave her daughter a stern look. "Are you ill?"

"I'm fine," Shu insisted. "Morgan, is there anything else we need to talk about?"

"Yes, actually. Our next order of business is…" My stomach growled again, and I amended my words. "To eat pizza. But while we do that, I want to tell you about Hazel. Do you realize that she's already immortal and has been body-hopping for millennia? She tried to get in mine—drawn to Caelus' powers and my youth—but I got away."

Miranda grew pale, and Lin blinked in surprise.

"I had no idea," Lin said. "Immortal? I didn't know that was even possible."

"That's what the elders are striving for," I said. "Mothers get extra power, elders achieve immortality. But Hazel doesn't need it. Instead, she's trying to release the Spirit elemental. A former lover, apparently, from eons back. It's a messy situation." I hissed a sigh then straightened my shoulders. "While that's interesting, it's not the crucial point. We have the Leaf and Seed back." I dug into my pocket and extracted the locket with its long, broken chain. I tied the snapped ends in a makeshift knot and draped the necklace over my head.

The others exclaimed with wide-eyed shock and joy.

"That's amazing," Miranda said, her dull eyes shining with the first glimmer of interest I'd seen from her in days. "Now we just need the Thorn. Should we destroy them now?"

Caelus' consternation echoed through my mind. He still wasn't sure if destruction was the best path, given the lies Air had fed him. I wasn't certain myself, so I said, "Let's keep them until we find the Thorn. We don't know if we'll need them to find it. This is all uncharted territory. Anyway, we have a more important thing to discuss. How can we get Joy away from the order? Any ideas, Shu?"

Shu's face brightened at my request for her thoughts. I chastised myself for not including the others sooner. I would need to vet any ideas they had, of course—someone had to corral them—but fresh perspectives were valuable, and the others enjoyed feeling listened to.

"Mum and I were talking about that, since Joy wasn't at any of the locations we checked out already." Shu followed me to the pizza and continued to talk while I chose a piece and brought it to my waiting mouth. "She has a good guess where they would have taken her. Beatrice has a pottery studio, but it's closed for renovations. We can look there right now."

"I can distract Beatrice while you extract Joy," Lin said. "I have order business that needs her attention. I can find some, anyway."

"I can get Joy's car," Miranda offered. "She has spare keys at her grandparents' house, I'm sure I saw them. It can be our getaway car."

"Good." I stood straight, pizza forgotten in my hand. A decisive plan galvanized me in a way that little else did. "Miranda will drive. Shu, I want you to get Amanda to check out the location before we arrive. We need to spread our resources, so we aren't accidentally spotted. Lin will text Shu when Beatrice is busy, and Shu and I will get Joy out and into Miranda's ride. Any questions?"

They shook their heads. Shu's eyes were shining with resolve, and she didn't seem to mind that I'd taken over her plan and improved it with some tweaks. I supposed it was still her plan in essence, so she was happy. Was that all it took?

"I can't wait to see Joy," Miranda said with a tremble in her tired voice. "I hope she's okay."

CHAPTER XIII

Miranda and I spent a tense afternoon pacing the little shed, waiting for Shu to get back to us. Finally, when the sun had set and dimmed the light shining through the shed's grimy window, the door creaked open. Miranda shuffled to it.

"Well?" She swung the door wide and ushered Shu inside. Did Amanda find Joy?"

"Joy is at the studio." Shu brushed her hood off her head then rushed to the window. She peered outside with quick, nervous movements, and her shoulders trembled. "I don't think I was followed, but I don't know. They're watching us all the time."

"Did you see someone?" I was instantly on high alert. Would we have to move locations again? The order had so many members that it could afford to keep a watchful eye on our movements.

Shu shook her head, her eyes still trained on the yard outside. "No, but I know they're there. Hazel has eyes everywhere. I don't think we should go out tonight. It's too dangerous."

I exchanged a confused glance with Miranda. Shu was usually the bold one. I could hardly hold her back yesterday when she wanted to rush in and liberate Joy as soon as we found her location. Why was Shu suddenly so cautious?

"We can't leave Joy with the order," Miranda said in a reasonable voice. "Who knows what they're doing to her?"

"Amanda said she didn't look good," Shu said absently.

"Then we have no time to waste," I said. "Call Lin and tell her to distract Beatrice."

"We need to find another way." Shu wrung her hands and faced us. Her forehead was furrowed with worry. "They'll capture us all, for sure. It's too dangerous."

"This is Joy we're talking about." Miranda put her hands

on her hips and stared at Shu. "We need to get her. I don't care how scared you are, you need to pull yourself together. Joy would do the same for you."

"Look at her temple," Caelus murmured for my ears only. "She's worked herself up so much that her threads are knotted. Try massaging them out and see if she improves."

"Shu," I said aloud. "Can I fix your hair? It's a little mussed."

Shu shrugged, and I moved forward before she could say no. With a few swift movements, I plucked apart the knot in her strands.

Shu's face cleared. "You're right. We need to get Joy now. I'll call my mum right away. Get yourself ready."

Miranda ambled toward the bathroom, and Shu pulled out her phone.

"That was effective," I murmured to Caelus when I turned to find my coat.

"A little too effective," he replied. "I didn't expect a complete change of heart, more of a mild relaxation."

I narrowed my eyes at the changeable Shu. She paced the shed again, unable to keep still. Something wasn't right with her, but I didn't have time to figure it out now. Joy waited for us.

When Shu's phone pinged a half hour later, we all jumped.

"My mother has Beatrice occupied for the next hour," Shu said. "Let's go."

Shu flew to the door with Miranda and me close behind. With our hoods up, we jogged to Joy's car—Miranda lagging behind—and piled in. It was fully dark now, and streetlights flashed through Caelus' thread-body and highlighted Miranda's face as she drove.

"It's the next block over," Shu whispered from the back

seat after a few minutes of driving. Her hands twisted in her lap. "Find parking soon and we'll walk."

"No sign of familiar threads," Caelus said quietly.

Miranda twitched at his voice. "I forgot Caelus was here. That makes me feel better. You and Shu won't be defenseless, even though you don't have any amulets."

"Shu can regularly take down all the sisters on the mat," I said, zipping up my coat. "But, yes, I admit that having Caelus on our side eases my mind as well."

Miranda pulled next to the curb in front of a closed clothing store along the quiet business section. She turned off the car and turned to us.

"Be careful," she said, her eyes big with worry. "Are you sure I shouldn't come with you?"

Her threads twitched with the apprehension that I would say she should come.

I shook my head. "Stay here and be ready to drive as soon as we get back. You're our getaway car."

Miranda nodded quickly, her relief clear. I put up my hood and exited the car. Shu joined me on the sidewalk and led the way.

Beatrice's pottery studio was down a side street. Its large glass windows gave a good view into the darkened studio, and a pair of motionless legs behind a pottery wheel made my heart jolt. I clutched Shu's arm.

"I see Joy," I hissed. "How do we get in?"

"There's a back door. Follow me."

Shu led me in a trot around the building, through a side parking lot, and to the back wall which more parking stalls nestled against. An industrial door waited for us.

"I have a lock-pick kit I borrowed from Amanda." Shu strode forward. I followed close behind, ready to wield my own lock-picking talents. When Shu dropped to the ground in a dead faint, I nearly tripped over her.

"There are wards, you fool," Caelus shouted. "Get away

before they send you to sleep, too!"

My eyes crossed, and I stumbled backward. The world spun around me in a dizzying spiral that threatened to pull me into blissful oblivion.

"Fight it," Caelus commanded. "Stay with me, Morgan. Don't you dare succumb."

I gritted my teeth and drew on my iron will. I would not fall asleep. That would mean the end of our mission, and I was not willing to let Hazel win.

Slowly, with enough effort to make me sweat, I pushed back the sleepy sensation. My eyes cleared, and my head stopped spinning.

"Shu's fading," Caelus said, urgency lacing his voice. He pointed at my fallen friend. "Look at her threads. The ward is sucking the life out of her."

I focused on Shu's tomato-red strands, and my heart squeezed. They were drifting away from her body like dye in water. It was a slow process, but undeniable.

"But I can't get to her," I said in frustration. "The wards are in the way."

"Get to work. Start with that line and untangle it from that thread."

Caelus pointed at the complex weave of threads that were strung in dainty lines through the air. Their colors were muted, barely glowing at all, but still I cursed my lack of observation. If I'd seen these, I would have stopped to examine them before we charged forward.

"Hurry," Caelus said. "She's fading."

"Any more I need to untangle?" My gaze swept frantically over the area. I tried to ignore the cloud of red strands expanding over Shu's motionless body.

"There." Caelus pointed. Once I'd leaped to the spot and massaged a knot out of the threads, they drifted away. Caelus bounced on my arm. "Go. Hurry. We stopped the ward's workings, but you'll need to gather her threads together before her heart stops, if it isn't too late already."

I dropped to my knees beside Shu. With one hand, I grabbed her wrist and checked her pulse. It was slow, too slow, and my other hand gathered red threads in a loose-fingered grip like a rake through leaves.

"Just press them into her body?" I asked Caelus.

"Get them close to her. She'll do the rest." Caelus pursed his lips. "I think."

"You *think*?"

I blew air through my own lips and pushed strands against Shu's stomach. At first my fingers on Shu's wrist detected no change. Slowly, after five sweeps of my hand through the air, her heartrate pumped faster and more powerfully. When the last of her strands found her body and clung to it once more, Shu gasped and sat up.

"What happened?" she said.

"Wards," I said shortly. "I took them down. Are you well enough to keep going?"

"Yes." Shu pushed herself to her feet and wobbled for a moment with her hand on her chest. "Yes, I'm fine. Exhausted, but good enough."

"Then stand back and I'll pick the lock." I gathered air threads and formed my handy serrated knife, then slid it into the lock and jiggled it around until the tumbler fell. My knife dissolved when I released the threads.

"Here." Shu passed me a black ski mask. "You want it? I bought some in case an order member is here. I don't want to be recognized, then I won't be part of the order anymore and no one will tell me any useful information."

"Good thinking." I considered the mask, then put it in my pocket. "But I'm already enemy number one, so I won't bother. You should definitely wear one, though."

I pushed the door open slowly. The entryway was as black as night, and even air threads didn't illuminate the space. Shu wiggled past me—clearly braver or more motivated than me—

and I followed cautiously.

A bulge of air threads moved toward Shu.

"Watch out," I shouted, but it was too late. A stream of multicolored strands jetted toward Shu in the dark. Shu shuddered, then she spun around. Lights flicked on, but I couldn't focus on anything except Shu's calm face as her hands reached toward my throat.

My instincts turned on, and I dodged to the side. The door slammed shut behind me, trapping the two of us in the entryway of the back of the studio. A shadowy figure stood in another doorway, but all my attention was taken up by Shu, who lunged at me again.

Shu was quick, and I hadn't exaggerated when I'd reminded Miranda that she was the best fighter of all the sisters. I'd only been learning their skills for a few months, but Shu had been training her whole life, and her dedication showed.

"She's being controlled," Caelus said as I batted away Shu's grasping hands. One landed on my wrist, and I twisted it frantically out of Shu's grip. "Thea's over there with an amulet. She must have had another control amulet made."

"That's only interesting in a theoretical way." I rolled on the ground to get away from Shu. I didn't want to hurt her, but she was making my mission a challenge. "What do you want me to do about it?"

"Get that knot." Caelus pointed at the tangle on Shu's forehead. "That's what the amulet did. That's how Thea's controlling her."

"Sure." I exchanged blows with Shu, backing up as the more experienced woman gained the advantage. "Let's sit down for a bout of untangling. That seems likely."

Shu hooked a leg around mine. I crashed to the ground, winded, and she leaped on top of me. Her face was still eerily calm. Her hands reached out and circled my throat before I could prevent her.

CHAPTER XIV

My air stopped, and panic licked at the edges of my mind. I scrabbled at Shu's hands around my neck, but her grip was relentless and unshakeable. I tried to kick at her, but my feet couldn't contact her back. I didn't have long before my brain stopped working.

"The threads!" Caelus shouted at me, his eyes wide. He jabbed at the knot with his finger. "Get the knot."

Caelus whooshed inside our body to force my hands, but I was already moving. My fingers took hold of the knot. I didn't have to completely unpick it. Any change in its configuration should release Shu. I hoped.

My fingertips squeezed the knot and smushed it around like a ball of clay. It disintegrated in my hand.

Shu blinked and released her hands from my throat with a horrified look.

"Morgan?" Her face crumpled with shock and guilt. "I'm so sorry."

I didn't waste time consoling Shu or even getting up. Instead, I gathered what air strands floated within reach and threw them at Thea. She stumbled and her amulet clattered to the floor.

I shoved Shu off me and threw another blast at Thea while I pushed to my feet. Thea braced herself against the hallway wall and glared at me.

"Get Joy," I yelled at Shu.

She scurried behind me. My hands gathered air.

"You're ruining everything," Thea yelled. Her eyes were wide with a rage tinted with madness. "But you won't succeed. The order is too powerful and our mission too important."

Thea dug in her pocket, but I threw my air ball at her before she could get another amulet. When the ball hit the older woman, she jolted then danced around in discomfort.

"The tickler," Caelus said. "Nice. Now, hit her with the snowball."

I lobbed Caelus' suggested air ball at Thea. Caelus and I had started naming our weapons for ease of use, and it was finally paying dividends. Thea's lips turned blue as her body shivered uncontrollably.

Despite her distraction, she pushed a shuddering hand into her pocket and withdrew a compact mirror.

"The eagle," shouted Caelus. "Send her flying."

I wasn't quick enough. Thea's amulet walloped me with the weight of a thousand bricks. I hit the ground, my lungs wheezing with the unaccustomed effort.

I felt rather than saw Shu dragging a barely conscious Joy behind me. I lifted heavy eyes to Thea. She tried to aim her shivering hand into her pocket once more, but her movements made it impossible.

"Knock the amulet out of her hand," Caelus said.

I directed a grumpy feeling at him through our connection. It was a good idea, though, so I gathered my strength and raised my hand off the ground. It was at glacial speed, and it took every molecule of energy I possessed, but I fought the weight until my hand raked through air. With a finger, I flicked strands at Thea.

The amulet flew out of Thea's hand and hit the wall. Instantly, my body lightened. I leaped up, my lungs filling with air, and dashed through the outer door before Thea could liberate another amulet from her pocket.

The others were outside, but not far away. Shu was almost dragging Joy down the sidewalk through a drizzling rain. I scooped Joy's flopping arm over my shoulders, and Shu and I pulled our friend down the street and toward the car.

Miranda pulled up closer when we came into sight. I yanked the door open and carefully folded Joy into the backseat. I climbed in after her, and Shu slid into the front passenger's side.

"Go," I said to Miranda, and she didn't wait for a second invitation.

Miranda drove with reckless haste through the quiet evening streets. The car's windshield wipers flicked back and forth like a metronome while Joy groaned in the backseat with me.

"Hold on, Joy," I murmured to her. "I'm working as fast as I can."

My fingers danced over the knots in Joy's threads that hovered above her wounds. I focused on the nasty gash on her arm first, as it looked on the verge of being infected. I started on her bruised head just as Miranda squealed to a stop on the street outside the mechanic's shop.

"Get her inside," Shu hissed at us. She leaped out of the car and wrenched open the back door. Miranda ran around to help, and together, they lifted Joy's unconscious torso out of the car. I followed with her feet, and together we stumbled to the shed.

Joy groaned again, but her head injury prevented her from regaining consciousness. Once we'd heaved her onto the bed, I knelt at her head and unpicked the knots at her bruise.

"Is it working?" Shu danced with impatience. I shook my head, keeping my eyes on my task.

"Boil some water," I instructed. "Miranda, find something that's easy to eat. Joy will need a warm drink and food when she's healed."

They scurried off to follow my directions. Caelus popped out of my arm.

"That worked," he said with mild admiration. "You got them to stop hovering."

"They needed something to focus on." I pursed my lips and nodded at Joy. "Can you give me a hand with this knot? It's a tangled one."

Together, Caelus and I smoothed out the worst of Joy's knots. When we were done, I sat back on my heels and surveyed Joy. Some of her bruising remained—I hadn't done a perfect job, but she would heal easily after this—but her face was calm, and she wasn't leaking blood anywhere.

Shu approached with a cup of tea, and Miranda pulled up a chair next to the bed with a piece of bread spread with honey.

"Is she okay now?" Miranda whispered. She lay her head on the bed and clutched Joy's hand.

"She will be." I pushed to my feet and stretched my arms above my head. "She needs to rest. When she wakes up, give her the tea and toast."

Joy moaned, and I swiveled to face her.

"Morgan?" Joy blinked at me, then looked around. "Miranda? Shu? Where are we?"

"You're in a safe place," I said. "We took you away from the order."

Joy's eyes filled with tears. "For real?"

"Yes." Miranda grabbed her hand and gripped it tightly. "You're safe, now."

"What did they do to you?" Shu crossed her arms and glared, but her expression wasn't for Joy. Her fingers clenched and unclenched her shirtsleeves convulsively, as if itching to pick a fight.

"They tried to get information from me." Joy blinked away the moisture in her eyes. "They wanted to know what we were up to, whether we knew where the Thorn was, what our plans are. I didn't tell them anything, except—" Her eyes sought mine for absolution. "That Morgan goes to the shops on Cormorant Drive frequently. And I might have slipped about your spirit. I'm sorry."

"You have nothing to be sorry for," I said firmly. "You did more than we could have ever expected you to. I should apologize to you. You wanted to leave the order, and I convinced you not to."

Joy shook her head. "You couldn't have known. Oh, I need to tell you, the last time Hazel came to me, she said that she was close to finding the Thorn. Like, really close."

She yawned, and her eyelids fluttered closed. I waved the others to the kitchen area away from the bed. They gathered around me, and I opened my mouth to speak.

The shed door creaked open, and I tensed, but it was only Lin. Her eyes flicked to Joy on the bed, and her relief showed in her expression and in her threads.

"You got her," she whispered, joining us. She gave Shu a one-armed squeeze. "Good work, everyone. And Beatrice didn't suspect a thing."

"She might now," I warned her. "Stay on your guard."

Lin straightened her spine, and her eyes hardened. "Let them come. They will find one mother who is not defenseless nor unprepared. Hazel may have her iron grip on the rest of them, but she doesn't have me."

Shu glanced at her mother with admiration. I hoped Lin's pronouncement was more than just bravado.

"Good," I said. "Well, this evening was a success. Joy is with us once more. But the fight is far from over. We're still no closer to finding the Thorn, and Miranda and I haven't been successful in making amulets. We made one, but it is embarrassingly underpowered. I don't know what went wrong."

"That's because the order doesn't make its own amulets," Lin said. "We outsource that job to someone who is far more experienced." At my incredulous look, she shrugged. "Making amulets is hard. Who has time for that? We just use them. Hazel portions them out according to our place in the hierarchy, but all the elders know the amulet maker. Let me do some digging tomorrow, see if I can find out more."

"Yes." I stared at Lin with growing respect. Shu had been right to bring her into the fold. Maybe now we could get somewhere with our missions. "We want amulets so that we aren't outmatched, should push come to shove. I presume someone would notice if you started helping yourself to the mothers' stash."

"Eventually," Lin said. "And the elders have more powerful ones, anyway. If you can get the amulet maker to make you elder amulets, you'll get a leg up, for sure." She looked at her daughter and held out a ring surrounded by threads. "Speaking of amulets, wear this one. You've been so jittery lately, I don't know how you can even sleep. This should calm you."

Shu slipped on the ring. The threads twined around her finger, then she nearly collapsed. Lin caught her under the arms and guided her to the couch.

"I'm exhausted," Shu groaned. She rested her head on her mother's shoulder. "What's going on?"

"The amulet must be working," Lin said, but her forehead creased. "Come on, I'll drive you home."

Shu and Lin took off a few minutes later with promises to keep us informed of developments. Miranda washed up then crawled into bed next to Joy, who slept peacefully beside her.

I dimmed the lights, but I was too wired to sleep. I checked the time on my phone. Jerome might still be at the bakery if I hurried. I knew he had a cake due soon. He would probably be working on it. Ever since his overbearing manager had been fired for helping himself to the till, Jerome had continued to use the kitchens at night worry-free to work on his cake decorating business, Butter & Scotch.

I shouldn't visit. Hazel might be watching the bakery. I shouldn't jeopardize Jerome's safety.

But I longed to see him. I'd told myself to give him time, let him come back to me if that was what he wanted, but I couldn't wait. I wanted to be in his presence, hear his low chuckle, watch his muscles move under his shirt.

And I wanted his advice. My path only grew rockier with every passing day. While the sisters were on my team, and I appreciated them very much, they weren't the same as Jerome. I didn't feel like confiding everything to them. I didn't feel like their equal. Sometimes their superior, sometimes their inferior, and sometimes on a whole other sphere of existence. Maybe, with time, we would grow to become better friends, but not today.

Today, I wanted Jerome.

If any sign of the order lurked in the shadows, I wouldn't approach. With that comforting decision, I waited until Miranda slept peacefully beside Joy. When all was quiet, I slipped on my coat and slunk out of the shed, opening the creaking door only enough to squeeze my body through. A light drizzle pattered down on my hooded head, and the tires of occasional cars that zipped by whooshed loudly against wet streets. A rust-colored pigeon sat in a nearby tree, watching me with beady eyes, and I smiled at the familiar sight. I don't know why Beaky had imprinted on me, but I appreciated the company.

I hunched my shoulders and marched toward the bakery. When I grew closer, I whispered, "Caelus. Can you help me check out the area? I want to make sure Hazel or the others aren't watching nearby. Joy told them I like going to Upper Crust."

Caelus ballooned out of my arm and perched on my shoulder. His thread mass blocked my view to the left, but his keen eyes swept the road and approaching alley.

"No humans around," he said. "A rat and your pigeon, but that's all. They might be watching Upper Crust, but probably not while it's closed. Did Joy tell them about Jerome?"

"I hope not." A shiver ran down my spine at the horror of that thought. I hastened my footsteps, eager to reach his side and make sure he was okay. "I don't think so, but I can't be sure."

I walked swiftly into the alley behind the bakery's shop row. In case someone was watching the front door, I would enter through the back.

"How are you getting in?" Caelus asked when I approached one of the numerous back doors between parking spots and dumpsters. "Will Jerome hear your knock?"

I raised my fingers and twisted silver air threads between them. After a moment, a serrated blade hovered above my palm.

"Back to our old tricks," I said. "I'm pretty good at picking locks these days."

The lock tumblers clicked, and I pushed the lever to enter. The shop row was set up similarly to the hallway behind Cut Right, the salon where some of the sisters worked and which housed their headquarters below. A long hallway ran behind the shops, with storage rooms and exit doors on the alley side.

"Which one is Upper Crust?" Caelus said.

"The one with the sign, I imagine." I pointed at a small plaque opposite us that spelled out the bakery's name.

Caelus huffed. "Yes, fine. Get on with your lock-picking, then."

I kneeled then stuck my blade in the door's lock. This lock was stickier than the outside door, but after a minute of fumbling, the click I was waiting for sounded in my ears.

"Wait, why am I coming in with you?" Caelus said. "Your interactions with Jerome are either dull or awkward for me." He crossed his arms. "Beaky isn't here, though, so I'm stuck."

"Just curl up in a ball and stay quiet," I pleaded. "Jerome is so jumpy around you."

"He is, isn't he?" Caelus chuckled. "But fine, I can be discreet."

He melted into my arm, and his silver threads coalesced into a glowing ball at my stomach. I unzipped my coat and smoothed my hair, inexplicably nervous. Then I straightened my shoulders, annoyed with myself. I was too old to be this hesitant.

"Pull yourself together," I whispered then pushed open the inner door.

The bakery was quiet, but a light over a counter lit the dark space. Jerome was bent at the waist, an icing bag in hand, piping edging on a towering black three-layered cake with a flowing river of white chocolate butterflies descending the side. His brow was furrowed in concentration, and his hair flopped over his forehead in a sandy lock that I wanted to brush back for him. He completed the bottom edge then stood back to admire his work.

"It's gorgeous," I said softly.

He jumped—literally jumped, his feet leaving the floor—then he whirled around, icing bag held at the ready like a weapon.

"What are you going to do?" I asked, amused. "Shoot sugar at me until I get diabetes? It's a rather slow form of self-defense."

Jerome sagged against the counter. "Morgan, you about gave me a heart attack. What are you doing here?" He held up his hand. "Never mind, it doesn't matter. It's good to see you."

"Is it?" I crossed my arms, unsure. Did he really mean it? "I didn't expect you to say that. Anyway, I'm here because— well, I missed you. And I could use your advice."

Jerome's face softened at my pronouncement, but he nodded gravely and put his icing bag down.

"Advice about what?" He pulled a large box closer to his work area and loaded his cake into it while he listened.

"Where do I begin?" I took a step closer to lean against the counter. "We got Joy back. Hurt, but alive."

Jerome whistled. "That's good news."

"It is." I sighed. "All my careful plans have fallen through during this elders debacle, and the only one that worked— rescuing Joy—was Shu's idea. Do you think I take over too much? Is there hope for me as a leader?"

"Maybe leader isn't the right word." He crossed his arms and tilted his head. "You say you're a team? Maybe coach is a better term. Someone who helps the others be their best but doesn't get in their way."

"I like that. Thanks, Jerome." I smiled at him, my eyes

touching on his features one last time before I left. I turned to go.

"Wait," he said. I looked back. Jerome rubbed his forehead. "Don't go yet. I want to say something. What you told me the other day, about—" He swallowed. "About your past."

"Yes?" I held my breath, anxious beyond measure about what Jerome would say next. It had been a very long time since I'd cared so much about what another person thought of me. It was painful, but in a necessary, life-affirming way.

"It's weird. I can't deny that. But I don't care." Jerome wiped his hands on a towel and stepped closer to me. His honey-colored eyes gazed into mine with intensity. "I like you, Morgan. Or whatever your name is. You're there for me in a way that no one has been since I was a kid. Your life is so bizarre that it keeps me on my toes." He huffed a laugh. "I don't care about Caelus, your history, any of that. I want you in my life despite that, maybe because of it. I want you, Morgan."

Jerome's raw exposure of his feelings for me cut to my core. My eyes moistened with my answering emotion, and my body heated pleasurably at his words.

"I'm so glad you said that," I said, breathless. "Because I want you, too."

I stepped into his waiting arms, and he nearly crushed me with his embrace. His lips met mine with hungry passion. I pressed into his body, my knees weak but his strong hands holding me up. His warm scent mingled with the sweetness of the bakery and made me dizzy with desire. I clung to him, desperate for more.

"I want you," I gasped. "I want you."

Jerome groaned. His hands grew frenzied at my hips, my breasts, my thighs. I pushed up his shirt to touch the skin over his taut stomach. He ran his hands under my thighs and hoisted me onto the counter with a swoop that made me shriek.

He grinned briefly then reached for the button of my jeans.

I sighed with pleasure. Then I glanced at the counter.

"This is so unhygienic," I said. "You make food on this counter."

Jerome paused, then he chuckled. "You really are an old woman. Unhygienic. Would it make you feel better if I promised to bleach the counter after?"

"You weren't planning to?"

Jerome grinned then covered my mouth with his to stop my words. That was fine by me. We had more important things to do than talk.

My zipper descended, then Jerome's warm hands slid into my jeans and cupped my upper thighs, lifting me up to pull off my pants. I clung to his neck, helping, pressing myself against his chest, needing to be closer to him.

BANG.

CHAPTER XV

Jerome's hands clenched on my legs. My head whipped toward the back door, and my stomach tightened. My first thought was that Hazel and her cronies had found us.

My ardor cooled like a candle doused in cold water.

"It was probably nothing," Jerome said, but his entire body was so tense I could almost feel him vibrate. "A cat on a dumpster, maybe."

"We should check, though," I said. "Just in case."

Jerome stepped away from me, and I slid off the counter and zipped up my jeans. We walked with quick but quiet footsteps to the back hall. At the outer door, Jerome paused and looked at me.

"Ready?" he whispered.

I nodded, my hands clutching silver strands in preparation. Jerome took a deep breath, gripped the door handle, and yanked.

Jerome stepped out first, but I pushed forward swiftly. Whatever was out there, we would face it together, even if it were only a cat.

Four men ranged in the alley, lit only by distant streetlights. Jerome's intake of breath told me that he knew them. For my part, I was relieved it wasn't Hazel and the order, but Jerome's tenseness didn't bode well.

"Jer," the front man said. He stepped forward, and his face caught the glow of the streetlight. My eyes widened. His similarity to Jerome was striking. They shared the same broad shoulders and build, the same strong jaw, and the same eyes. But this man's eyes were piercing in an unsettling way, and the lines of his face were hard without any of Jerome's warmth. Tattoos snaked over his hands and neck and promised more under his leather jacket.

He looked like what Jerome could be in twenty years with

a different life. I shivered. Jerome's father was dead, but was this the uncle he said had raised him after his parents' demise at age eleven?

"Brant," Jerome said in a constricted voice. "What are you doing here?"

"You're not an easy man to track down." Brant took a box of cigarettes out of his pocket and extracted one. He placed it in his mouth and waited for the man with a goatee next to him to light it. He took a drag, his eyes never leaving Jerome's face. "I shouldn't have to. You should have been my welcome-home party when I got out. Why didn't you come to me when Tiny called you?" His eyes narrowed, and Jerome shifted his feet. "Why did he come back with broken ribs instead?"

I glanced at Jerome. Had his clearly thuggish uncle been incarcerated? Had Jerome beaten up his visitors? Suddenly, Jerome's secrets the past week made sense.

"That life is over for me, now," Jerome said roughly. He cleared his throat and said louder, "I've started new. I don't want to be part of your gang anymore."

Brant spat. "That's the thanks I get," he growled. "You're lucky I took you in. I could have left you for the foster system, but no, I gave you food, clothes, a family. I taught you more than your soft father ever would. I don't know what my sister was thinking when she married him." He pointed at Jerome with his cigarette. "I gave you everything. I made you my second. And for what? So you could turn your back on me?"

"I wish you had left me in foster care," Jerome said bitterly. "I didn't want the life you gave me. I didn't ask to be your second. You groomed me into the position and never asked me what I wanted. When they busted you, I saw my out and I took it."

Brant flicked his cigarette to the ground and stepped forward. His face pulled into a sneer.

"You're too good for us, is it?" He laughed without mirth, and the men around him chuckled darkly. "You didn't mind when that drug money was paying for your new street bike. What, now you have some little job that follows the rules, you clock in, get your paycheck, clock out?" Brant took another step forward, and his men gathered behind him. "You're going against family. Betrayal from my own flesh and blood?" He shook his head. "Not on my watch."

Jerome shivered. I stepped closer to him until we were almost touching. The pull of his uncle's magnetic force was almost tangible on Jerome, and it was clear that Brant had been an overwhelming influence on Jerome for years.

"Come on, Jer." A man with a shaved head and a scruffy leather jacket held up his hands in a pacifying gesture. "We're all friends here. We're practically family. Come back with us and have a drink. I'm sure you like your new little life." He glanced pointedly at me. "But we can remind you of the good times."

"And what you owe us," Brant said in a low, menacing tone.

Jerome was silent for a long moment. I glanced at him. His eyes were downcast, and his jaw worked. His threads drooped and twisted around his body in a protective manner. Brant had a firm grip on his nephew, and Jerome was having a hard time shaking it. Brant's leadership was clearly controlling in the extreme, and I reflected uneasily on my own leadership with my team. I hadn't been nearly as bad as Brant, but maybe I'd been too far along that spectrum for comfort.

"I don't owe you anything," Jerome said, but his tough words were contradicted by a warble in his voice.

"If you're not with us," Brant said, lifting his chin. "Then you're against us."

The men with Brant widened their stances, and their strands tensed in preparation. Shaved Head who had spoken earlier shook his head in sorrow but prepared with the others.

I gripped Jerome's arm. "I'm with you," I said in a fierce whisper. "I've got your back."

He threw a disbelieving glance my way. The pain in his eyes made me want to throw my arms around him, but we had no time for embraces. He searched my face and then nodded.

Goatee and a man with a hooded sweatshirt ran forward. I stepped away from Jerome to give him space and readied my air balls. Intense relief swept through me that Caelus wasn't flying with Beaky right now. His power thrummed through my body, and his approval at my choice of attack filled my mind.

I let the first air ball fly at Hoodie. Hoodie tripped forward as his legs flew out from underneath him, and he slammed into the ground with force.

Goatee was occupied with a punching, grappling Jerome, and from the grunts of concentration, I gathered Jerome was doing just fine. I focused on Hoodie, who leaped up with surprising speed given his fall, and Shaved Head, who approached me with wariness in his hooded eyes.

"Don't know what weapon you've got, lady," he called out. "But you should leave while you still can. This doesn't concern you."

"If it concerns Jerome, it concerns me," I replied. My fingers spun threads together in a practiced motion. "And you should leave while you still can."

Hoodie took a switchblade out of his pocket, released the blade, and threw it at me with vengeful accuracy. I neatly dodged the flying knife and released my air ball at the man. He patted his chest with increasingly frantic motions, trying to put out the fire he assumed was there. It was only heat, but he didn't know that. Shaved Head rushed forward, and I shoved my other air ball in his face. It also burned, and Shaved Head yelled as his eyes squeezed tight against the sensation.

"Incoming," Caelus yelled.

A body slammed into my side, and I hit the pavement with a jarring jolt. My teeth clacked together, and I narrowly missed cracking my head on the asphalt. Heavy breathing scented with cigarette smoke and alcohol filled my face, and the man bent at the waist and pushed against my shoulders.

"You're a feisty one, aren't you?" Hoodie said with a sneer. "I can see why Jerome likes you."

I bared my teeth at him. "You'll regret this," I said. "Sooner rather than later."

My hands weren't free, but air powers weren't my only trick. I brought my leg up and kneed Hoodie in the groin. He stumbled sideways, his face contorted with pain, and I leaped to my feet.

This had gone far enough.

"Caelus," I panted. "Take over for a second. Guide me in making a big enough wind to blow them all down the alley."

Caelus' thread-form disappeared, and an instant later, my arms moved under his direction. Swiftly, he gathered silver threads. A recovered Shaved Head stalked toward me, Brant watching with another cigarette in his mouth. Jerome was still grappling with Goatee. When a surge of intention flooded my mind, I screamed.

"Jerome, push him away!"

With a grunt of effort, Jerome braced his legs and shoved the other man as hard as he could. Goatee stumbled away, then a gust like a semi-truck hit all four of the other men. They flew off their feet and landed near the road on the opposite end of the alley.

I raced to Jerome and pulled him to sit behind the dumpster. We didn't have long—the others were down but not gone— but I needed to make sure Jerome was okay. I scanned his body for major injuries, but aside from a few bruises and cuts, he appeared unhurt.

"Why are you helping me?" he said. His eyes searched mine. "Now that you know the truth? I've done terrible things in my past."

"Join the club," I said. "Once, I almost killed a woman in cold blood for power. Not my finest moment, and one that I truly regret. You," I jabbed his chest, "are more than your past.

You were only eleven when your life was chosen for you by your uncle. You didn't choose him, but guess what? You chose the life you have now. That was all you. And you can choose to ignore Brant now, stand up to that terrible influence who has controlled you for years. You can make your own decisions now and decide the course of your own life."

Jerome breathed heavily and stared at the wall opposite. Fire kindled in his eyes.

"You're right," he said finally. "I don't have to put up with him anymore."

"Of course I'm right," I said. "Are you ready to put your new-found determination to the test? Because I hear them coming back."

Jerome nodded. I squeezed his hand, then we jumped up and spun around each side of the dumpster.

"Hit them with everything we've got," Caelus said, his eyes sparkling with excitement. "Try the screwdriver and the tornado."

I grinned and gathered the necessary threads. Goatee charged at me, clearly unaware that I'd been the one to throw him and his cronies down the alley. Shaved Head approached me more cautiously, and Hoodie aimed his ire at Jerome. He must have learned his lesson earlier.

I let the tornado fly first. It hit Goatee in a roaring swirl of air. It tossed him off his feet and twisted him in a sickening spin. When the wind died and dropped him to the asphalt, I followed up with the screwdriver. Goatee's skin erupted in painful red lesions that looked like nothing more than someone attacking him with a screwdriver, hence the name.

Shaved Head backed away, clearly torn between following Brant's orders and wanting to run away from the crazy lady with magic powers.

Jerome punched Hoodie in the cheek. Something cracked, and Hoodie fell to his knees and clutched his face. Jerome looked down at him for a moment, his expression indecipherable, then he walked toward Brant.

Brant stood straight. "You think you're ready for me? I've been fighting since before you were born. You don't have the guts to attack me."

"I don't want to fight you," Jerome said, his voice clear and steady. "But that's the only language you understand."

Without warning, Jerome punched Brant in the stomach. The older man stepped back, but not quickly enough to completely avoid the blow. He doubled over, but swiftly recovered and slammed a punch in Jerome's side. Jerome wheezed then threw himself at his uncle.

The flurry of blows that followed made me bite my tongue until it bled, but I didn't step in to help. Jerome needed to prove something—to his uncle, to himself—and me getting in between him and that goal wouldn't help anyone. I was ready to jump forward the moment Brant had the upper hand, but it hadn't happened yet.

Finally, Jerome landed on top of his supine uncle with both hands on Brant's forearms. When Brant lifted his head and upper torso with a growl of rage, Jerome smacked his forehead against his uncle's. Brant's head fell to the pavement, stunned. Jerome stood and towered over the fallen man.

"We're done," he said quietly. "You will never come after me and mine again. Ever. Do you understand?"

Brant stared at him with glazed eyes. Jerome kicked his side.

"Do you understand?" he shouted. Brant gave an approximation of a nod. Jerome walked away from his uncle, ignoring the slack-jawed other men. He pressed the small of my back and steered me toward the bakery back door. I let him, as eager as he was to leave the presence of Brant and his gang.

When the door closed, I put shaking hands on Jerome's cheeks and drew his face closer to mine.

"You did it," I whispered. "You broke free. Is that what's been bothering you lately? The secret you haven't wanted to tell me?"

He nodded, his eyes miserable. I shook his head gently.

"I meant what I said outside. The past is a murky place, and I am the last person to pass judgement for wrongdoings. If there's anyone who believes in fresh starts, it's me. I don't care what happened before. I care about who you are now."

Jerome took a shuddering breath, his expressive eyes never leaving mine. His arms wrapped around me, then suddenly he was kissing me, pressing against me, practically crushing me in his adrenaline-strengthened arms.

I ran my hands through his hair, forcing him closer, even though there was no space between us. It wasn't close enough. The high of battle was too much to resist. Jerome twisted us so my back was against the wall, and I rubbed my hands over his shoulders.

He cried out in pain then quickly stifled it, although his threads remained tight.

"You're hurt," I said, releasing him to examine his wounds. "I'm sorry, I should have healed you first."

"I didn't give you much of a chance," he said ruefully. He breathed heavily, but the knots above his wounds were clearly visible now that I was looking. He sighed. "Maybe we should do that first. If we're going to—" he swallowed. "Well, I'd like to do things properly."

I rubbed his firm chest, as eager as he was, but willing to see his point.

"Fine," I said. "Healing first. But don't think I'm not coming back to collect on that promise one day."

"I'm counting on it," he said.

CHAPTER XVI

It was hard to sleep that night, with the adrenaline from the fight with Jerome's uncle and my desire for Jerome left unslaked. Once I'd healed Jerome's wounds, we'd both descended from our adrenaline highs, and he'd driven me back to the shed. I finally gave up my tossing and turning on the uncomfortable couch at five in the morning. I felt impotent and stuck in this one-room shed without clear directive. Joy was back and healed, but artifacts and amulets were out of reach.

I still had my fledgling business to attend to, so I sat at the table with my papers surrounding me and got to work charting a marketing course of action for a shoe store at the far end of Cormorant Drive. When I had something to show, I painstakingly typed it out on my phone and sent the document to a local copy shop. It opened at eight, so I would jog there to arrive as it opened then deliver my plan to the shoe store.

I felt better after completing my task. I might not be able to do anything for our mission right now, but I was still useful.

Joy and Miranda continued to sleep, so I grabbed a granola bar and slipped on my runners. Hooded coat firmly in place, I jogged toward Cormorant Drive. I tried to take a circuitous route to avoid detection, and I was panting by the time I arrived at the copy shop. Caelus rotated above my head, searching for familiar threads in every direction.

After my deliveries, I ran back along Cormorant Drive. I passed Upper Crust on the opposite side of the road. I desperately wanted to stop—my whole body yearned for it, Jerome, lemon tarts, and all—but I couldn't allow myself to submit to temptation. For all I knew, someone was watching the doors of the bakery, waiting for me to slip up again. I was certain Hazel hadn't given up on her quest to take my body for herself.

When I returned to the shed, Miranda and Joy were awake

and eating cereal. Lin had joined them, and she stood when I entered.

"I know where to find the amulet maker," she said without preamble. "We can go today. Right now."

I blinked at her. She stared back, waiting for my reaction.

"Great," I said. "I'm ready when you are."

Joy half-rose from the table, but Lin gently pushed on her shoulder to make her sit again.

"Not you," she said. "You need to rest. Eat. You're so pale."

"I agree." I looked critically at Joy, who was a shadow of her usual bubbly self. "Miranda, will you stay with her?"

"Of course," she said, pouring Joy some more tea. "I'm not much use anywhere else. Go get us an amulet so we can take the order down. No one should mess with my sisters and get away with it."

Lin drove us in her crossover to an area southeast of Chinatown. The streets were grungy, and the buildings had seen better days.

Lin parked behind a beat-up panel van, and I exited the car with trepidation. Caelus emerged from my arm.

"The order doesn't pay the amulet maker well, I'm taking it," Caelus said.

"Is that the elemental possessing you?" Lin's eyes searched my body. Caelus' threads were invisible to her, of course, so her eyes eventually sought mine.

"Caelus, meet Lin," I said. "Lin, Caelus. Now, which way to the amulet maker?"

"It's a block away." Lin raised her hood over her immaculate black hair. "I didn't want to give us away if someone is watching. Follow me."

Caelus scanned the streets for familiar threads while I

walked in Lin's footsteps down the street, past a pawn shop and a dispensary, and around a corner. Lin finally stopped at a dingy alcove with buttons beside a wooden door. She pressed the third button up, and a buzzing sound traveled into the busy street.

"Yeah?" A young, female voice answered eventually.

Lin leaned forward. "I'm from the order. May I enter?"

A different buzz answered Lin, and she pushed the door open. I followed her into a hallway dimly lit by a grimy window at the landing of the staircase before us. Lin stepped upward without a word. My footsteps were quiet on the threadbare carpeting, but the wooden treads creaked underfoot.

Two doors emerged at the third-floor landing. Without hesitation, Lin knocked at the rightmost one.

The door swung open. A young woman stood before us, holding a bowl of chocolate-flavored breakfast cereal. She wore an oversized sweatshirt over a pair of pink pajama pants with unicorns on them, and her hair was pulled up in a messy ponytail. She gazed at us curiously through large, hooded eyes above full lips that held in her crunching.

"What's up?" she said through her mouthful. "I don't recognize you two. New in the order?"

"Something like that." Lin pressed down the front of her coat. If she were anything like me, she wanted to straighten the woman's sweatshirt and run a comb through her hair. "May we come in and speak with you further?"

"Of course, of course." The woman stepped back and held a hand to her mouth. "Sorry," she said after she swallowed. "Milk everywhere. I'm Naomi, by the way. I make all the amulets for the order."

"I'm Morgan," I said absently. My gaze was caught by the room I found myself in. The clutter made my tidy side itch with cleaning urges, but my curious side drank in the excess. Shelves lined the walls, filled with mismatched jars of powders and strange shriveled items. A large open-topped pen on the far side housed a fluffy rabbit chewing alfalfa and two long-haired guinea pigs who squeaked on occasion. Long tables took up much of the floorspace and were covered with papers, glass containers with liquids inside, and bizarre items like a pile of sheep's wool and strips of tree bark.

"You haven't seen us before." Lin stood on the side of a table covered with beakers and vials, clearly unsure where to sit and deciding against it. "Because we are here for a secret project."

"What, is it someone's birthday?" Naomi heaved a pile of grungy animal pelts from a stool onto the floor and flopped onto it. The stool swiveled with her motion.

"Not exactly." Lin glanced at me, and I took over.

"Do you know what the order does with the amulets you make?" I asked.

Naomi raised her eyebrows in her surprise. "No. I just love making them. It started a few years ago. I'd found some old books in the archives at the university that described magical processes. Of course, I dismissed them the first time I read them, but they were so intriguing to read that I snuck them home. One night, I'd had too much to drink, and I tried one out." Her large eyes opened even wider until she resembled an owl. "And it totally worked. I turned purple. Like, royal purple. So cool. So, I started making more. I told a few friends about it, but they didn't believe me, and they always explained away what I did with ridiculous mundane excuses."

"How does the order play into this?" Lin asked.

"They found me one day." Naomi swiveled her chair. "Another student started chatting me up, then she showed me recipe pages from an old book she had. Obviously, I was so excited. When I told her more about what I'd done, she wanted me to make her some magic objects. She called them amulets. I've made a ton for them now, and they do all sorts of things." Her eyes brightened. "When I get a new recipe, that's the best. It's so fascinating. And they pay decently, too, enough for me to set up my lab here.”

Naomi swept her hand around the room, clearly proud of her workspace. She had a point. If I overlooked the terrible clutter, there were interesting items here. Naomi’s hand hovered over vials of viscous liquids, rods of various metals, and fluffy cotton clumps.

“So, you have no idea what they use amulets for,” I said to clarify. “It’s all academic to you. A proof of concept if you will.”

Naomi narrowed her eyes at me. “What are you getting at?”

What do you think, Caelus? I said in my head. *Is this woman telling the truth as she knows it?*

Her threads say so, he replied. *Are you going to trust her?*

I tightened my lips. That was the question. Could I relax my grip on this amulet conundrum enough to let a stranger in? I wanted to make the amulets myself—I wanted to do everything myself—but I’d found out recently that I wasn’t always the right person for the job. Forcing my way on others hadn’t solved anything, and it wasn’t until I’d listened to Shu’s ideas that we’d rescued Joy. I needed to trust a little, and delegate what I couldn’t handle myself.

“The order has questionable tactics, and even more questionable motives,” I said. “Evil is a strong word, but they might be approaching it. They’ve used your amulets for manipulation, coercion, and even torture. Their ultimate goal is to find the Thorn, an extremely powerful artifact that will give them even more power.”

Naomi’s eyes grew round again, and she set her bowl of cereal on the over-full table without looking at it.

“No,” she whispered. “I didn’t think—they seemed so nice. Why would they do that?”

“They have their reasons,” Lin said crisply. “Not good ones, though. We want to stop them from releasing an apocalypse of biblical proportions upon the world, but we are outmatched without amulets of our own. Will you make us some so we stand a chance?" She pulled out her wallet and pulled out bills. "We can pay you."

I was glad that Lin had offered to pay. While my first check had cleared the other day from my newest client, most of that money had gone toward stocking the shed with groceries.

Naomi stared at Lin's wallet, then she shook her head vehemently.

"No," she said. "No, put away your money. I'll make you amulets without pay. I need to make amends." She looked at us with hard eyes. "But how do I know you're not the evil ones, misleading me with your words?"

"You don't." I nodded with approval. "Finally, you're learning the value of thinking critically. Unfortunately, you need to decide that for yourself."

Naomi gripped the edges of her stool with white knuckles, caught in her dilemma.

Caelus emerged from my arm again. "We have plenty of proof for you," he said. "But not a lot of time. So, if you could move past your existential crisis and help us out, that would be great."

Naomi looked around the room wildly. "Who is that?" she gasped. "Who's there?"

"That's the elemental spirit who shares my body," I said. "He's right, though. Time to make up your mind."

Naomi stared at me for a long moment, then she jumped off her stool and ran to a bookshelf nearby. She pawed through the trinkets on its shelves, frantically searching for something. Finally, she held up a pair of glasses in triumph. They were blue tinted sunglasses with rhinestones glued to the rims.

"Aura sight." She smashed the glasses onto the bridge of her nose and looked my way expectantly. "I spelled it to visualize the magic layers. Ah, ha! There you are."

Caelus and I glanced at each other in surprise. No one could see Caelus except for me, and a light of interest kindled in Caelus' eyes. After all his snobbery about amulets, here was something that finally piqued his interest.

"Amulets aren't totally useless after all, are they?" I teased.

Naomi stepped forward eagerly. "Wow, so nice to meet you. What's your name?"

"Morgan calls me Caelus," he said with hesitation. He waved his hand in Naomi's face, and she flinched. "You can really see me?"

"Clear as day." Naomi beamed at him. "I have so many questions for you."

"Before we get into question period," I said, pulling copied pages of the Book of Souls out of my pocket and presenting them to Naomi. "Can we get started with making amulets now?"

Naomi took the pages from me, her greedy eyes scanning the words rapidly.

"I never get to keep the recipes," she said. "Obviously, I've written down what I can in my own notebooks, but this is great. Yes, I have most of the stuff I need for these. I could use some turmeric for this one, though. I don't work until this afternoon, so I can get started right now." She glanced at me. "Can I chat to your spirit while I work?"

"You'd better ask him," I said. I didn't have anywhere to go right now, so I might as well watch Naomi's methods and learn a thing or two. I was curious about where my own amulet-making process had gone wrong. "I'm not in charge of who he listens to."

Lin said goodbye and left to buy turmeric. I elected to stay in the epicenter of clutter and magic since Caelus was keen, and I wanted to watch Naomi work.

"Start with this recipe," I said, unwilling to hand off all responsibility to the younger woman. I might be learning to delegate, but that didn't mean I wanted others to run rampant. "And I could use a place to sit, if you have one." I glanced pointedly at her mess of a workspace.

Once Naomi had uncovered a chair for me, I settled in to

watch her work. She kept her ridiculous glasses on, and Caelus drifted as close as he could to her workspace. Between the two of them, they produced a constant barrage of chatter. Naomi was fascinated to learn about Caelus' world and how he manipulated his element, and Caelus was no less interested in her amulet workings. After a few minutes, I tuned them out and watched Naomi's hands instead.

Above a motley assortment of items—crushed sage leaves, a crucifix on a golden chain, a vial of what looked like empty air, and a fabric bag filled with rice that Naomi heated in her microwave—Naomi's hands danced with precise movements. She hummed on occasion while she did it, and threads from her items drifted upward and wove through her fingers and with each other. Before long, a seething mass of multicolored strands gathered in a cluster below her hands. With a sudden movement, she flicked it down to a metal Christmas ornament in the shape of a star. The strands latched onto the object, and Naomi dusted off her hands. Caelus looked impressed and immediately praised her for her deft movements.

I could replicate her practiced motions over time, but it would take a lot of work. Maybe Hazel had the right idea to pay Naomi for her services.

With that conclusion, I looked around for something to do. Being amid all this clutter made me itchy and irritable. With half a glance at the absorbed duo, I stood and walked to a nearby table. It was covered in clutter. I gathered loose papers into neat piles, lined up equipment along the back edge, and swept loose powders into a garbage can. When I finished the table, I moved onto the bookshelf, leaving tidiness and order in my wake.

"Amulets have their place." Caelus' voice drilled into my subconscious as I dusted a bookcase's top shelf. "But have you ever thought about making artifacts?"

"I thought those could only be done with a combination of spirit and humans working together," Naomi said.

"And what do you think we are?" Caelus crossed his arms. "We could totally make one."

"Excuse me." I put my hands on my hips, more surprised than annoyed. "Is this the same elemental that's been whining to me for months about removing all artifacts from the physical realm, they don't belong here, they upset the balance, blah blah blah? When did you change your tune?"

"When Air told me to focus on the Leaf, Seed, and Thorn," Caelus said with heat. "When I realized there was a whole other element that I never knew existed. When Air hid things from me. Do artifacts truly upset the balance, or is that something that Air told me to make me look for those three artifacts without telling me about Spirit? What else has Air lied to me about?"

"Artifacts have been in the world for centuries," I said slowly. "The ones we've found and destroyed were ancient. If the balance was off, nobody noticed."

"Exactly." Caelus huffed with indignation.

"I'm totally up for experimenting." Naomi held up the metal star. "But for today, your amulet is ready."

I took the star from Naomi and examined it. Its threads were tight and coiled with precision, far more elegant than the amulet I'd tried to make.

"What does it do?" I asked.

"Say the trigger word 'star-nosed mole' when I tell you to." She ran to the wall and flicked off the lights. The room was plunged into darkness only alleviated by a crack of light emitting from Naomi's closed bedroom door. Her voice called out, "Okay, say it."

"Star-nosed mole," I said, feeling foolish.

Threads burst out from the ornament and wrapped around my head. The room brightened so much that I assumed Naomi had flicked the lights back on, but the quality of light was odd. Everything was outlined in a strange glow, and the colors were more washed out than usual.

Naomi grinned. "Helps you see in the dark." She flicked the lights back on and the odd effect faded. "Pretty cool, right?"

"Perfect." My lips curled in a smile. I tucked the amulet in my pocket. "Thanks, Naomi."

Footsteps tapped on the stairs, and we swung our heads toward the door. When Lin entered with a grocery bag, we all relaxed.

"Great." Naomi rushed to Lin and grabbed the bag. "My turmeric. Look, come back tomorrow morning and I'll have more amulets for you, okay? I promise, I'll do whatever I can to help against the order. I hate being taken advantage of, and I hate feeling stupid more. They're going down."

CHAPTER XVII

Lin dropped me off at the shed. It was well after lunch, and I was starving and ready for a sandwich. When I pushed the shed door open, a cacophony of sounds greeted my ears.

"Morgan!" Joy dragged me further into the room. "Look. Denise has joined us, too. Amanda brought her into the fold. Isn't that great? There are so many of us, now."

Denise smiled at me, her big brown eyes wide and innocent. "I hope you don't mind, Morgan. I want to help. The order has gone too far lately. They need to be stopped."

I gazed at Denise, my mind working frantically. Her cream-colored threads twisted around her body in an odd juxtaposition to her calm demeanor.

Caelus, I said silently. *Is she on our side?*

She's definitely hiding something, he said. *Watch your back.*

"So good to have you here," I said warmly. "We are growing into a force to be reckoned with. Have you seen how well Joy is doing after her terrible ordeal?"

Denise's threads squirmed again, but her back straightened. Her empathy for Joy's plight was fighting something, maybe her loyalty to the order? The more I looked at Denise, the more I grew convinced that she was a mole.

"Yes, it's such a relief," Denise said, and this time, her threads didn't show a lie. "I was worried about her when I heard. This is a nicely hidden spot you found, Morgan. How did you manage it?"

"Oh, a friend of a friend lent it to me," I said, deliberately not naming names. "But what's the news from the order?"

"Yeah, we're looking for—" Joy began, but I interrupted her.

"Any details you have that might be useful," I said smoothly. I handed Denise a cup of water from the counter.

When she glanced at the cup in confusion, I glared meaningfully at Miranda, Joy, and Amanda. They looked startled. I hoped that was enough to warn them to keep their mouths shut around Denise until I could speak to them further.

"Well," Denise started. "I don't know much—the sisters never do—but I did hear from one of the mothers that Hazel and Beatrice are so close to finding the Thorn. Like, we're preparing for the final ceremony to join all three artifacts together. Hazel has us checking through our amulet inventory to gather the most useful weapons to guard the area."

"Wow," I said. "They're that close? Where are they planning to reunite the artifacts?"

"No idea," Denise said. "I heard someone talking about a lake, but that's all I know. I'm still a trusted order member, though, so I can do some digging."

"That sounds perfect," I said. "Look, why don't you go right now and see what you can learn about the location. The rest of you, stay here while I assign you your tasks for this afternoon." I ushered Denise to the door. "I'm so glad you joined us, Denise. We need all the help we can get."

Once Denise had wandered back to the road—closely watched by me through a grimy window—I turned to the others.

"Amanda," I hissed. "What the hell were you thinking?"

"What do you mean?" Amanda's blue eyes were wide with shock and the beginnings of anger. "I vetted her carefully. We need more members willing to go against the order."

"She played you like a fiddle." I paced the small area. "She's still loyal to the order, clear as day. Never mind. It just means that we'll have to move. Again. Hazel will know where we are, now."

"We have to leave?" Miranda sank into a chair. "Where are we going to go?"

"We'll have to get a hotel room." I sighed, long and heartfelt. I didn't have the money for that, and neither did any of the sisters. "I guess that's why they invented credit cards."

I strode up to the hotel's front desk like I owned the place. A little confidence went a long way in most situations.

"I'd like a room, please," I said to the clerk. "Your best price."

"Of course." The woman in her fitted vest and blouse tapped at her computer. "I'll need a name."

I pushed my credit card across the counter. "Put me down on the ledger as Jane Smith if you will. Keep my real name out of the equation as much as you can."

The woman glanced at me with a twinkle in her eye.

"It's like that, is it?" She tapped at her keyboard some more then produced a keycard for me. "Room three-eighteen is available for you, Ms. Smith. Enjoy your stay."

I nodded my thanks and waved the other two to follow me. Joy limped, and Miranda clutched the hamster cage in tight fingers. We all looked more bedraggled than I wished, and I looked forward to a proper shower.

This hotel in downtown Vancouver wasn't the priciest, but it was clean and comfortable. I couldn't justify an exorbitant fee, but I was tired of living in a dusty shed. I would have to worry about my credit card debt after this debacle was over. I hated being in debt to anyone for any reason, but desperate times called for grinning and bearing it.

After I threw up some hasty wards over the room's door, Joy sank onto the nearest bed when we entered the plain but serviceable room with two queen-size beds and a small desk near the window. Miranda dropped her bag and leaned against the wall.

"This is our new home, is it?" she said listlessly.

I snapped my fingers at her. "None of that attitude. We had a set-back, but we also have too much going our way to sink into despair. We'll all take showers, then we are going to comb the Book of Souls again for hints of the Thorn's whereabouts. Denise's clue about lakes was a great start. We have Joy back, and we have Naomi making us amulets. We can do this." I clapped my hands when Miranda continued to lean against the wall. She jumped. "Go on, take your shower, Miranda. Chop, chop."

Miranda shuffled to the bathroom, and the sound of running water drifted through the closed door a minute later. Joy rested on her side, her face still pale, while I spread the Book and our papers on the small desk.

After we were all clean and as fresh-faced as we could be under the circumstances, I gathered the others around the desk. Joy sat on the edge of the bed, and Miranda perched on an upturned garbage tin. I spread my hands on the desk from my seat on the only chair.

"Denise let slip that Hazel focuses on searching around lakes." I flipped to a page in the elders' section of the Book of Souls and pointed at the dense text there. "I think she got the idea from this section, the most recent text from explorers fleeing the Old World to set up their goddess worship in North America. The text mentions the power of water for protection, but it doesn't give an exact location." I drew the Book closer to me and grabbed the translated page tucked inside. "I'll read you the section."

Our goddess must be worshiped under the living trees she adores. The Thorn of her blessed Tree is our talisman and our connection to her. We must protect it at all costs and worship her as she deserves. For she is the goddess of life, of everything that grows and lives and dies. Barren wastelands are abhorrent to her. The Thorn must be held where all can keep it safe, where all can touch its greatness, where all the parts of the world can join to cradle it in safety. It will lie by the calm water that all life needs.

"The calm water that all life needs," Joy repeated. "That's

pretty clear. Seawater is too salty to drink, so not all life needs it." She rubbed her face. "I'm sorry, my brain just isn't working today."

"Ocean animals can drink seawater," I reminded her. "But if we consider that the author of this text held a land-centric view of the world, which I believe we can, then fresh water makes the most sense. 'Calm water' indicates a lake, or at least a slow-moving river."

"Which is why Hazel has been searching the wilderness all these years," Miranda said, leaning forward with interest despite her moroseness. "Looking for the right lake, I guess."

"But where would these goddess-worshipers leave the Thorn, if they wanted everyone to keep it safe?" Joy leaned back on her hands, her brow furrowed. "And what does that even mean? How can everyone keep something safe? It seems like an unlikely wish."

"You three are such humans." Caelus whooshed out of my arm. His voice startled the other two, but I looked at him with interest.

"Enlighten us, Caelus."

"You were complaining about the author being land-centric before," he said with a smug look on his face. "But you're being very human-centric right now." At my expectant look, he sighed. "Come on. 'All the parts of the world can join'? Clearly, it's in a location where all four physical elements are present. Find somewhere where earth, water, air, and fire coexist."

"That's not entirely unhelpful." I nodded at Caelus in appreciation, and he rolled his eyes at me. "Water is easy enough to come by, if the Thorn is placed near a lake."

"Air is everywhere," Caelus said. "I should know."

"And so is earth." Miranda twisted her mouth. "But what about fire?"

"A volcano?" Joy suggested without much hope in her voice. She rubbed her head again. "Maybe they made some sort of eternal flame. Is that possible with an amulet?"

"I don't know," I said slowly. "But I find it doubtful. Even a magical fire must need a fuel source, surely. And five hundred years is a long time to burn."

"Assuming it's still burning," Miranda said darkly. "If the fire portion is gone, how will we find the Thorn?"

I stood and paced the small area in front of the window, unable to keep still while I was thinking. Caelus drifted along with me.

"What in nature has fire threads?" I murmured. "Let's think. Forest fires, but they don't last very long. Volcanoes, same thing."

"What about radioactive metals?" Miranda asked. She leaned her head against the wall. "Sometimes they're hot, and they can be found in nature."

"Yes," Caelus said with a look of interest. "That could work."

"I pity the poor worshipers, though," Joy said with a shudder. "Gathering around a radioactive shrine can't be good for your health."

"Still, they wouldn't have known about the health issues five hundred years ago." I crossed my arms and tapped my fingers on them. "Good idea, Miranda. What else?"

We were silent for a long moment. Joy's face was screwed up in concentration, and Miranda stared out the window, her eyes unseeing.

A brilliant brainwave crossed my mind. I stopped in my tracks, and Caelus floated in front of me with a quizzical expression.

"Hot springs," I gasped. "Heat from the earth. Long lasting. Would have been around five hundred years ago."

The others' eyes widened.

"Yes," Joy breathed, her cheeks pinker than I'd seen since before we'd rescued her. "It's perfect. Harrison Hot Springs is so close. How could it be anywhere else?"

"I'm sure there are other hot springs around," I argued, but inside I was as elated as Joy. It all fit. The Thorn was almost in our grasp. "First thing tomorrow, let's pick up our amulets and drive to Harrison."

CHAPTER XVIII

Miranda whipped out her phone. "I'll text the others," she said, her thumbs a blur on her screen. "There, Amanda knows the plan. Now for Shu. Shu can tell Lin. This is so exciting."

"I can't believe it," Joy said in a dreamy voice. She flopped back on the bed and stared at the ceiling. "My whole life, I've been longing for this day. All three artifacts!" Her expression grew thoughtful. "I know we won't join them, and the promised utopia is a sham, but still. That we actually found all three is huge. Ugh, my head. It's like brain fog and a hangover all in one."

I peered at Joy more closely. Tucked behind her left ear were a few dainty threads that didn't match her violet strands.

"Caelus," I said quietly. "Do you see anything off about Joy?"

Caelus emerged from my arm and peered at my friend on the bed.

"Now that you mention it." Caelus pointed at Joy's neck. "How did we not notice her amulet before?"

I paced over to Joy and pointed at her ear. Her left earring, a large hoop of gold, was loosely wrapped with muted strands of various hues.

"It's not an amulet." Joy touched her earring defensively. "They were a present from a friend, ages ago. Nothing to do with the order."

I touched one of the threads with a finger.

"It's changing her mood," Caelus said with a shake of his head. "I could sense it when you touched the threads. Carefully pull them off, and we'll see how she feels."

I pulled the strands gently from Joy's earring anchor.

"Better?" I asked.

Joy sat up and blinked. "Way better. What did you do?"

"You must have been affected by an amulet." I mashed my

hands together. "The order must have been behind it." My eyes landed on Miranda. The desk was the only thing stopping her from collapsing to the floor in her funk.

"Her necklace," Caelus said. "Get those threads off."

I stepped toward Miranda and plucked the strands off a simple chain that clung to her slender neck. When the last one dropped to the floor, Miranda's back straightened.

"Let's get the Thorn right now." Her eyes glinted with life and vigor. "What are we waiting for?"

Joy and I glanced at each other.

"We'll get there," I said finally. "But we also need to figure out how you two had threads of amulets on you. The ones on your necklace were changing your mood, making you depressed. Do you have any idea where that came from?"

"No." Miranda frowned and touched her neck. "Not at all. I must have been close to someone in the order. But I've been hiding ever since we stole the Book of Souls."

"Maybe the threads were activated from afar," I suggested. "Is that a possibility, Caelus? Could the order have turned on Miranda's despair-threads once they realized she wasn't on their side?"

"It's possible," Caelus said.

"But it's all gone now, right?" Miranda felt her neck again.

"Wow, that's subversive," Caelus said. "Miranda felt overwhelming despair and Joy couldn't think or hardly move."

"What about Shu?" said Joy. "She was so jittery, at least until her mother gave her that calming amulet. Do you think she was infected, too?"

"Stands to reason." I rubbed my arms, thinking about how Hazel had wormed her way into our team without my knowledge.

"Subversive," Joy said slowly. "That's the sort of amulet the elders favor, so I've heard. They can get into your mind and twist things."

"The order is too good at planting them," I said. "I suppose they did yours when you were captured. I should have noticed before."

"You got it now before it could do much damage," Joy consoled me. "That's what matters."

"You know how we should celebrate our freedom from the order's magic?" Miranda leaped up. "Let's go shopping. I have no clothes that are worthy of artifact hunting."

"And what, pray tell, do artifact-hunting clothes look like?" I stared at Miranda, amused. "Besides which, money is tight, especially after paying for this room."

Miranda waved away my objections. "I saw a secondhand store across the road. And, I don't know, something sturdy. Boots would be a start. Who knows what we'll encounter out there? What if the Thorn is booby-trapped?"

Joy glanced at me in concern, and I sighed.

"Fine, we'll go shopping. But only across the road. We've kept under the order's radar so far. Let's keep it that way."

After we pulled up our hoods and donned sunglasses, Miranda led the way through the hotel's lobby and across the street. True to her word, a large secondhand store waited for us. Once inside, Miranda made a beeline for the shoes, and Joy wandered to a rack of pants. I walked down an aisle lined with coats of all descriptions—bright purple ski jackets, long trench coats, even a sequined vest—and my fingers ran along the sleeves of each one. They stopped at smooth black leather. I pulled the garment out. It was a fitted leather coat with strap details that pulled the look together to turn a plain coat into something stylish and youthful.

My mouth quirked. It was too funny imagining March in something like this, but Morgan would fit it perfectly. I slipped off my current coat and shrugged on the new one.

It slid on like a well-fitting glove, supple and worn-in. I zipped up the front, and a feeling of invulnerability stole over me.

"Yes." Joy looked at me with admiration when she wandered my way. "Love it. You look badass. It's super sturdy, too. Good for whatever booby traps might be at an artifact location. Find me one?"

We flipped through the racks until both of us were outfitted in snug leather jackets. Miranda opted for a sturdy raincoat and hiking boots that would leave a mark if she kicked too hard. I paid for my purchase, happy to have a layer of protection for whatever lay ahead. Leather might help a little, but the confidence it brought would do more.

We returned to the hotel in high spirits with our purchases and a bag of pho takeout. We were kitted out for anything, we had two artifacts and a lead on the third, and we were picking up amulets tomorrow. I tried to inject a realistic note to my giddiness, but it was difficult. The other two didn't even try, and it was late before we all settled down to sleep.

The next morning, I rose early and rousted the others out of bed.

"I want to pick up those amulets and get going to Harrison," I said, shaking Miranda's shoulder to wake her. "The sooner we get this done, the sooner we can go back to our regular lives. Without artifacts, what purpose would the order have in pursuing us?"

"Assuming we destroy them," Caelus muttered to me.

I frowned at him. "Are you still chewing on Air's omissions? Even the Book made it clear that joining the artifacts would bring upheaval and destruction to Earth."

"But what if Spirit should be released? All I'm saying is that we don't know the whole picture."

"Let's get our hands on the artifact," I said firmly then shook Joy's shoulder. "Then we can debate this issue. Until we have the Thorn, it doesn't matter."

Joy groaned but shuffled to the bathroom without speaking. Miranda groped for her clothes.

"What amulets do you think the amulet maker made?" she

mumbled, peering at her shirt to find the front.

"Good ones, I hope." I laced up my boots. "Elder-style ones. I want to keep up with the order, and that means the big guns."

By the time we were ready, all three of us were dressed for anything. Miranda handed us belts.

"I found these at the shop," she said with a look of proprietary pride. "I thought we could hang amulets off them. Assuming Naomi made enough for that."

"Perfect." I buckled my belt through my jean loops. Extra holes with metal loops dangled from the hips. I had no idea what the original owner had used them for, but I could see their uses now. I patted the locket around my neck that held the artifacts and glanced at the silver cluster that was Caelus. I was as ready as I would ever be. "Got your car keys, Joy? Then let's go."

A knock on the door startled me. We glanced at each other, stricken, until I crept to the door and looked out the peephole.

"Amanda." I swung the door open. "It's just you. We worried when we heard a knock."

"Sorry to scare you." She gave me a tight smile.

I frowned. "How did you know we were here?"

"I told her," Miranda said. "She's one of us, after all. Our team."

A prickle of foreboding ran down my spine. I deliberately hadn't told Amanda, Shu, and Lin our newest location. The fewer people who knew where we were, the less likely something like Joy's capture would happen again.

But they were part of the team. If I didn't trust them, who could I trust?

"Shu and Lin are waiting downstairs in their car," Amanda said. "But I just wanted to wish you all good luck."

"You'll be there, too," I reminded her.

"Of course!" She looked scandalized, her pale eyebrows rising up her forehead. "I wouldn't miss finding the Thorn for anything. This is historic. But still, I wanted to give you all a hug."

Amanda clasped me briefly then moved to Joy. She lingered with Miranda and whispered a few quiet words to her. When Miranda nodded, Amanda released her.

"See you there," she said and left.

Naomi's building wasn't far. Joy took a few minutes to find parking, and when we finally pulled up to the curb, I leaped out and strode quickly down the sidewalk. A feeling of urgency stole over me. I wanted this whole Thorn business done. We could destroy the artifacts—assuming that was what Caelus wanted—and then I could move on with my new life and wash my hands of order business for good. It was all-consuming, this mission to tear down a corrupt secret organization. I was ready to move in a new direction.

Naomi flung open the door at my first knock. Her hair was even more of a tangle than yesterday, and she was wearing the same sweatshirt. Her eyes were tired but glinted with a manic edge.

"I stayed up all night working on your amulets," she said.

"I couldn't tell." I stepped inside her workshop and ushered the other two in. "Any luck?"

"Oh, yes." Naomi turned to her table and scrambled at its surface. She whirled around with a handful of metal objects. "Here. All top-tier stuff. You'll love them. This one?" She held up a keychain depicting a maple leaf. It dangled and gleamed in the soft light of Naomi's lamp. "It amps up your physical strength. And this one, man." She gazed reverentially at another keychain, this one with a purple flower. "It protects against amulet use. They're all keychains because that's all I could afford at the shop down below."

I glanced at Joy and Miranda, who both looked as

impressed as I felt. Caelus whooshed out of my arm and silently regarded the objects.

"We'll be unstoppable with amulets like those," Joy whispered.

"Ah, but the elders have the same ones." I gingerly took the flower keychain from Naomi and examined its illustration. "But it means we won't be squashed like bugs, should we come across an elder now. Maybe it finally means we won't have to stay in hiding anymore. This one protects, right?"

"Absolutely." Naomi held up another metal key ring. "Pair it with this keychain, and the elders will be hard-pressed to break it, unless they have one of these." She held up another. "But I've only made one of them for the elders, so your chances are good."

"We can go home," Miranda whispered. "I can go to classes again, see my friends. Did you make enough of the protection ones for all of us?"

"I have two." Naomi scrubbed her face and blinked a few times. "That's all I had time for."

"You and Joy can take them," I said firmly. "I have Caelus on my side, remember?"

"Is he here?" Naomi said eagerly. She groped in an overflowing basket nearby and came back with her ridiculous glasses. She smashed them on her face and looked our way. "Hi, Caelus."

"Your amulets aren't half-bad," Caelus said. "Not quite artifact-worthy, but pretty good for a human."

"I take that as a high compliment." Naomi beamed at him.

I snorted. "Well, it's probably the best you're going to get. Teach us how to use each one, and then we'll be on our way to collect the Thorn. I don't expect to meet much resistance, but you never know how the artifact might be protected. Every amulet you give us is a help."

Naomi held out the amulets one by one and rattled off their uses and the trigger word associated with each. I portioned them out between the three of us, and we affixed each one to our belts. I felt a bit ridiculous with items dangling off my waist like a massive charm bracelet, but the thought of the powers they bestowed on me was enough to make me swallow my pride.

"Can I try one out?" Joy said with hesitation. "So I know how it works?"

"Maybe not the pain-enhancing one," I said. "I'm not volunteering to be your guinea pig, anyway. What about the blinding one?"

Joy touched a resin-coated keychain and stared at me.

"Wombat," she said.

My vision tunneled, and I gripped the table's edge to steady myself. I'd known the blindness was coming, but it still threw me off balance. My heart thundered, and I had to regulate my breathing to prevent it from spiraling out of control.

"It's working," I choked out.

A light thud of something hitting the wooden table brought light back to my life. I took deep, shuddering breaths. Losing a sense was a shock to the system. Even through my distress, I marveled at the power we now held. At least we would be able to fight the elders on their level.

Once the blindness had retreated fully, I turned to Naomi.

"I meant to ask, why the choice of trigger words? I mean, wombat?"

Naomi shrugged. "It's a good idea to choose words that you aren't likely to come across in regular conversation. Hazel always wanted ancient languages, but since these amulets are for you, I decided to go for a modern flair."

"Fair enough." I clipped the final amulet onto my belt and straightened my new leather coat over the ensemble. "Latin can be hard to remember. Okay, we're ready to go."

"Wait." Naomi pushed away from her table and ran toward a door at the back of the workshop. A bed with tangled sheets was visible through the open doorway. "I want to come with you. An artifact like the Thorn? That would be amazing to see."

"I don't think—" I started, but Joy put her hand on my arm.

"Why not let her come?" she said. "She's already proven herself extremely useful with the amulets. She deserves to have a reward for making them all for us pro bono."

I wanted to say no, but Joy's pressure on my arm made me shut my mouth. I was trying to not put my foot down for every single detail of our little team. Was the request such a big ask that I couldn't agree to it? Naomi would be, at worst, a tagalong. At best, she could remind us how to use our amulets in sticky situations. Joy had a point.

"Okay," I said at last. "You're right. Let's bring her."

Naomi rushed back a minute later in jeans and a sweater, her hair in a marginally tidier ponytail. She grabbed a coat from a cluttered table and shrugged it on. I saw ten pockets in the canvas garment before I lost count, most of them secured with a protective flap. It clinked as she moved.

"What's in there?" Miranda asked, leaning forward for a better look.

"Amulets," Naomi said. "Of course. I bought this jacket specifically for the pockets. Okay, I'm ready."

We traipsed down to Joy's car, and Miranda and I bundled into the backseat while Naomi sat next to Joy in front. It was freeing to hold so many powerful amulets on my person. I didn't feel invincible, exactly, but a measure of confidence suffused me in a way that I'd been missing ever since Hazel had tried to exorcize Caelus out of me. I'd been living with low-grade fear for days, and I wasn't sad to see it go. I might not be able to waylay every plan Hazel had for me, but now I had a fighting chance. Between the amulets, Caelus, and my team, we were ready to get this Thorn and destroy it once and for all.

Miranda's phone rang before Joy pulled into traffic.

"It's Shu," she announced. "I'll put her on speakerphone."

"Miranda," Shu gasped through the tinny speakers. "Hazel called the order to meet her at Harrison Hot Springs. She found out somehow, I don't know. I swear, I didn't tell her."

CHAPTER XIX

My heart sank to the base of my spine. Either Hazel had figured out the clues at the same time we'd done so, or we had a mole.

"It doesn't matter now," I said firmly. "Our mission remains the same, but now we have a few more obstacles. We're on our way to Harrison right now."

"We'll meet you there," Shu replied. "Since we're called to come anyway, it won't look suspicious."

Shu hung up, and Joy and I exchanged a worried glance.

"It wasn't me," she said.

"Me neither," Miranda piped up from beside me in the back.

"I don't believe it was either of you," I said. "But, like I told Shu, it doesn't really matter. We're all going to Harrison anyway. Whatever side everyone is on will shake out once we're there."

Caelus floated out of my arm and stared first at Joy, then at Miranda.

"There's something off about Miranda," he announced.

Miranda looked affronted.

"Caelus," I said. "Why would you say something like that? Surely you know by now that humans don't like hearing that sort of thing."

"Really look at her," he insisted. "Look at her threads."

Naomi whipped out her glasses and peered at Miranda. I glanced up and down at her mustard-colored threads.

"What are you looking at?" Miranda said, crossing her arms. "It's just me."

"You're right, Caelus," Naomi said slowly. "Morgan, check out the strings at her left temple. See how they're all squiggly?"

I leaned closer. Sure enough, a cluster of threads was

snarled into a knot above Miranda's left eye.

"What does it mean?" I reached closer and touched the strands for Caelus to get a better sense. He scrunched his brow in concentration, then his eyes widened.

"Hold her down," he instructed. "Quickly."

Miranda's eyes flashed, and she reached for her belt of amulets. I was quicker, thanks to my trust in Caelus. With one hand, I threw air strands at her for distraction and pushed her hand away from her belt. With the other, I fashioned one of my air balls and shoved it in her face.

Miranda's eyes squeezed shut, and she clawed at her head blindly. The air I'd thrown at her enveloped her head in a roaring storm of wind that filled her eyes and ears with too much stimulation.

While Miranda was occupied, I twisted the strands of her feet and hands with those of the car. When she was secure, I batted aside my air ball attacking her then shoved a ball of air into her mouth. It would stop her from speaking but not breathing. I leaned back in my seat, winded from my exertions.

"What the hell was all that about?" Joy said, anger coloring her voice. "What did you do to Miranda?"

"She's being controlled," I said. "I don't know how or when, but she's not herself. Someone in the order is pulling her strings."

"Is she the mole?" Joy said tremulously.

"Maybe." I glanced at Miranda, who glared at me from above her air gag. "It seems likely now. But when did they have contact with her?"

"Can you fix her?" Joy said in a shrill voice so unlike her usual one.

"Not easily." Caelus examined the threads at Miranda's temple with a shake of his head. "It's complex. I don't even know where to begin, at least not without hurting her."

"What do we do with her?" Naomi stared at Miranda like she was a particularly fascinating zoo animal.

"Leave her in the car while we find the Thorn," I said. "No need to add to Hazel's ranks."

The car ride to Harrison was long and tense. As soon as we started driving, I texted Jerome to tell him what was happening. He deserved to know where I was, especially if things went south. I checked Miranda's bonds frequently, and Caelus glared at her the whole way. It was a wasted expression since she couldn't see him, but it made him feel better, if the grim satisfaction pulsing through our bond were any indication.

Naomi fiddled with her pocket-filled coat, and Joy drove with both hands clenched on the steering wheel and her jaw tight. Miranda wiggled occasionally but desisted when I glanced at her.

"You're not going anywhere," I said to her. "Not now, and not when we park. You're going to stay here and try to shake off the compulsion. It's technically possible if you have a strong enough will."

Miranda narrowed her eyes at me but didn't grunt through her gag.

We finally reached the highway turnoff to Harrison Hot Springs. We passed a carved wooden sign for the town above a freshly planted flower bed on this early spring day. Joy drove down the main drag—the town contained only a few thousand people—and pulled into a parking lot at the lake's edge. The lake was rumpled with wavelets from a chill breeze that swept down from the forested hills that surrounded it. Joy parked and turned to face the backseat.

"Will Miranda be okay in here?" she asked with a tremble in her voice.

"She might get a little chilled, but nothing too serious." I unbuckled myself and opened my door. "Don't fret, Joy. Let's get the Thorn, then hopefully we can figure out a way to break her compulsion. We have Naomi on our side, after all."

"That compulsion magic is strong," Naomi said. "Especially the elders' one. But nothing is unbreakable with enough work."

"There you go." I stood from the car and stretched my arms above my head then looked around to spot the others. "Joy, do you see anyone?"

"I see their cars," she said. "Still warm and ticking. They aren't far ahead."

The three of us shut our doors. I walked around to Miranda's side and opened her door a crack.

"We'll be back when we can," I said to her grumpy face. "Hang tight."

I straightened and moved to push the door closed, but Miranda was faster. She kicked the door hard with her leg, and it caught my side.

I wasn't prepared for the motion, and it flung me to the pavement. My cheek grazed the asphalt like a peach over sandpaper, and I cried out in pain. Joy and Naomi shouted, but Miranda must have done something with the amulets she'd somehow reached, because their shouts morphed into shrieks.

"Get up, Morgan," Caelus yelled at me.

I brought my hands under me, but a boot landed on the small of my back and pushed me to the ground again. Fingers fumbled at my neck, and a sharp tug broke the delicate chain of the artifacts' locket that I'd been wearing since I'd stolen it from Hazel.

"Got it," Miranda said with smug satisfaction. "You think you're so clever, so powerful. Like you've got us all under control. Didn't do you much good, did it?"

Is that how Miranda saw me? Or was that the opinion of whoever spoke through her? Had I released my stranglehold on the team too little, too late?

The boot pushed hard into my back, and I wheezed.

Miranda leaped away and ran through the parking lot.

"Amulets!" Caelus howled. "Air. Anything!"

I grabbed random silver threads and threw them after the retreating woman, but they did little more than ruffle her hair. Naomi shouted one of her ridiculous trigger words, but Miranda merely stumbled and kept running. My fingers clutched an amulet at my hip, but when I mouthed the trigger word, my battered diaphragm wouldn't cooperate to give me air. I coughed, and with every moment that passed, Miranda drew further away.

Miranda was gone, her mind taken over by the order. A moment of clarity alerted me to the truth. Miranda had chosen to tell the rest of the team where our hotel was, then Amanda had whispered a trigger word in Miranda's ear when they'd embraced. Amanda was the mole. Had she been the whole time? Part of me was impressed by the younger woman's deception. She had always seemed like an open book.

The loss of Miranda was a terrible blow, not only because our small team was down a member—two, counting the betrayer Amanda—but because she was a friend. I hoped we could free her before the order treated her the way they'd treated Joy.

I'd trusted the team, hadn't made Miranda swear our location to secrecy, believing that the team members' need for autonomy was more important than my tight control over everyone. If I'd forced my way, Miranda would still be with us. Was my bowing aside to their ideas and opinions worth her loss?

My breathing finally caught up to the needs of my oxygen-starved body, and I pushed myself to trembling knees. Everything ached, and my ravaged cheek stung like it was soaked in vinegar. My hand went to my empty neck, and I cursed. Miranda had taken the amulets. Now, Hazel had the Leaf and Seed and was well on her way to getting the Thorn. Spirit was about to be released to the world—accompanied by destruction I could hardly imagine—and I didn't know how to stop it.

My head whipped around to the others. Joy helped Naomi up from the ground. Both were breathing hard but looked mostly unscathed. Whatever Miranda had hit them with hadn't lasted.

"Miranda took the artifacts," I said, dusting off my new coat that was already scuffed with dirt from my fall. "We need to get moving. Oh, and Amanda is the mole. Text Shu and Lin to be wary."

A truck roared up the street and veered into the parking lot. Once it parked, Jerome jumped out of the cab and raced over to me. His coat was open, and it exposed the neck of a regular tee shirt. Unlike his usual buttoned-up polo shirts, this revealed the tops of multiple tattoos. My stomach squirmed happily. Jerome must have come to terms with his past after confronting Brant the other night.

"I'm here," he said. "Wait, what happened? Are you okay?"

I flung my arms around him. His warm scent enveloped me, heady notes of sugar and bread wafting in my nose like a bouquet of comfort, and I sighed.

"Better now." I disentangled from his arms. "But our allies are few and far between. Amanda and Miranda are with the order now, so all we have are us four, Shu, and Lin. Amanda was a mole for the order, and she turned Miranda with an amulet. It's my fault. I shouldn't have let Miranda tell Amanda where we were. I should have been more suspicious."

"You're not to blame," Jerome said gently. "You let her make her own decisions, that's all. You can't control people too tightly. They need the freedom to do their own thing, make their own mistakes. You have to trust them. Sometimes they'll get it wrong, sure. But sometimes they'll surprise you."

I closed my eyes and let out a shuddering sigh. Jerome was right. Miranda's compulsion wasn't my fault, nor my responsibility. Letting Miranda make her own choice and forge her own destiny was the right thing to do, even if it had backfired on us. I hoped we could save her before it was too late.

Pounding footsteps made me whirl around. Shu and Lin approached, their eyes wide with questions.

"We're here," Shu panted. "What's happening?"

"Amanda turned on us," Joy said in a choked voice. "And she put a compulsion on Miranda. They're both gone, and the Leaf and Seed with them."

Shu gripped her hair, and Lin whistled.

"So, this is the dream team?" Lin said in her precise voice. "And the rest of the order is between us and the spring head. Not to mention a small army of townsfolk that Hazel has compelled to protect the area. The odds are against us."

"What's the plan?" Shu asked. All eyes trained on me.

I took a deep breath. "I was going to ask you the same thing. You have insight into the order and their current plans. What do you think we should do?"

Shu looked surprised but gratified by my words. Her brow furrowed with furious thinking.

"We should split into teams," she said finally. "If some of us are captured, at least the others can have a fighting chance of getting through."

"And we can spread out the amulets," Joy said. "Everyone should have something."

"Good idea." Shu nodded at her sister. "I'll pin the spring head's location on your phone maps, so you know where to go. We'll all take a different path to the hot spring. Incapacitate anyone you meet."

"But don't forget the townsfolk are innocents," Lin reminded us. "Do your best not to hurt them."

I pursed my lips. This task was growing more difficult by the second, and we needed to get moving. Who knew how close Hazel was to retrieving the Thorn?

"Does three teams work?" Joy glanced around then pointed

at us in turn. "Shu and Lin, you two can stick together. Naomi and I will be a team, and then Morgan and Jerome."

"And me," said Caelus. "I'm amazingly useful, I'll have you know."

"And Caelus," Joy said with a gracious nod.

"Jerome and I can take the main path," I said quickly. Just because I was giving the others a say in what happened, didn't mean that I couldn't take the path most likely to be an issue. I was still the most competent of everyone here. "The other two teams can circle around and approach the spring head through the woods. Here, let's divvy up the amulets."

Lin already had some decently powered amulets, since she was a mother of the order, so we portioned our amulets out to the rest. Naomi described what each one did and told us the trigger words that would release their powers. Even Jerome got some after I insisted. I needed to know he would be protected and ready for anything, since fists weren't going to cut it for every situation. He held a keychain up with a dubious expression.

"That's a protection one," I said. "Take it, it won't bite. And this keychain will send your opponent to sleep when you say 'wooly bear' with intention. It only works once every five minutes—needs to recharge—so use it sparingly."

Jerome took the offered keychain gingerly but pocketed it all the same. Then he pulled out a switchblade and handed it to me.

"I know you have magic," he said. "But there's something comforting about knowing you have a real weapon."

I gripped the cold metal in my hand. It was a solid weight, and in some bizarre way, it did comfort me, mainly because it was Jerome's and he wanted me to have it. He was here, with me, and that was everything I wanted.

Well, that and Hazel brought to heel.

"Get Naomi to sharpen that blade with magic," Caelus said.

"I can totally do that." Naomi reached out her hand for the

blade.

I handed it over with hesitation. "Right here, right now?"

Without answering, Naomi whipped out an amulet from one of her many pockets and muttered over the knife. Her free hand twisted threads until a thin sheen of them clung to the blade. With a grin, she handed it back to me.

"Thanks." I examined the blade, then sheathed it and turned to the others. "Is everyone clear about their route?"

"What's the plan when we get to the spring head?" Lin said crisply. "Whoever is nearest will try to overcome Hazel? Should we wait for others?"

"If you have a chance, take it." I glanced around, and the others nodded in approval. "We're flying blind, here. Use your best judgement, and let's get those artifacts out of the order's hands."

With that, we took off at a jog toward the woods. Jerome and I stayed on the main path that meandered around the lake, while the others peeled off into the wooded hills beyond the town.

Almost as soon as Joy's bouncy blond hair disappeared into the forest, a crowd of townsfolk appeared around a bend in the path.

CHAPTER XX

The townsfolk blocked our way, their blank faces strangely menacing. A heavyset woman wearing jeans, a young boy with a scooter, a large man with a rolling pin, and a woman in a bikini were at the front of the group. We slowed our approach.

"Now what?" Jerome muttered to me.

"Wind, of course," Caelus said. "Blow them over, Morgan."

I brought my fingers up and swept the air until silver threads collected in my palms. Mindful of Lin's comment about the townsfolk's innocence, I didn't make my blast as strong as it could have been.

Nevertheless, the wind that barreled down at the row of people knocked every one of them to their backsides. I grinned at Jerome.

"Is that all Hazel has to throw at us?"

We marched forward, but the townsfolk leaped to their feet. Their faces were still eerily blank, and they rushed us as a group.

"Blast them again," Caelus shouted. I brought my hands up but didn't manage a handful before they were on us.

"How innocent are they, exactly?" Jerome yelled as he punched the shoulder of a beefy man wearing an apron from a nearby restaurant. "It's not easy to go light."

"Do your best," I shouted back as I wriggled out of a large woman's arm around my neck. I yanked her airway threads and she backed away, choking, but two more rushed me. Before they reached me, I yanked at silver threads.

My body rose with dizzying speed until I was above the townsfolk's heads. The two chasing me looked up with their blank faces. Were they pondering how to get me down, or were their thoughts as empty as their expressions?

I didn't wait to find out. My fingers pulled more silver

threads, but this time I aimed an airball at the two figures reaching their grasping hands toward me. A swirling column of wind blew my hair around my face and tossed the two against each other and to the ground where they lay groaning.

"The tornado," Caelus said. "Nice one."

"Thanks." I glanced down. Jerome was occupied with two opponents but didn't look in any real danger. I took a moment to admire the strength in his movements.

Many of the townsfolk were off their feet at this point, but a man in a plaid shirt walked toward Jerome. Two against one was bad enough, but I didn't like the odds of three to one. I didn't have time to construct an air ball, so I tweaked the silver threads holding me up and dropped to the ground in front of the man.

He was on me before I could prepare, seemingly unfazed by a woman dropping from the sky in front of him. He bowled into me, and we immediately grappled. Despite my self-defense training with the sisters, I was still far lighter and weaker than this lumberjack. However, I had Caelus and I had amulets. I touched my belt.

"Amethyst," I gasped. The man loomed over me. His arms slackened, and he slumped toward me in a faint.

I landed hard on the path with the man's deadweight pinning me down. My elbow crunched into a poorly placed rock, and I growled in anguish.

Another townsfolk ran toward me, this one a young woman with a jaunty ponytail and a lifeguard outfit too cold for today's temperatures. I struggled to get out from under the lumberjack, but she climbed on top of her fallen comrade and trapped me underneath. Pain jolted through my damaged elbow, and I gritted my teeth. Would the amulet work again, or did it need time to recharge like Jerome's sleep amulet?

I put my hand on another amulet, thought hard, and spoke the trigger word.

"Gecko."

The woman's movements turned glacially slow. Her eyes gazed at me in horror, but her arms would take ages to reach me or to push herself off the other body.

Great. Now I had two bodies pinning me to the ground, and I could hardly breathe for the weight of them both.

Jerome threw his last opponent to the ground, where the man lay groaning. He breathed hard and ran a hand through his hair.

"Jerome," I wheezed. "A little help here."

His head whipped toward me, and his eyes widened. He threw himself to my side and tossed the two bodies like they were sacks of flour in the way. He dropped to his knees and cradled my upper body.

"I'm fine," I said, both amused and touched by his concern. "I hurt my elbow, but that's it."

Jerome glanced at the injury, and his expression grew grave.

"It looks bad," he said. "Can you fix it?"

"No time," Caelus said. "Fiddle with your threads while you walk to get rid of the pain, maybe. But we need to keep moving if we want to stop Hazel before she takes over the world."

"Right." With Jerome's help, I rose to my feet, wincing at the shooting pain stabbing my elbow. My hand on his waist came back slick with red blood. "You're bleeding."

"It's fine." He moved further away. "Let's find this spring head."

"I'm healing you while we walk." I scooted to his injured side and grabbed knotted threads above a surface wound on his side when he tried to walk away. He winced and slowed his pace. "I'll just make it stop bleeding, remove some pain. I can't have you slowing down on me."

"Do your elbow first," he ordered. "You can't do anything without your hands."

"And you can't do anything without your blood," I

countered, but my good hand crept to my bad elbow and massaged the knots there.

We continued to walk forward at a slower pace. Once the pain in my elbow was lessened enough to think clearly, I tweaked a few threads on Jerome's side.

"Grab that one, there," Caelus instructed. "Then he won't lose all his blood. Humans are just bags of liquid, aren't they?"

Jerome chuckled. "Essentially."

A crashing sound in the woods stiffened my back. I grabbed a handful of air threads in one hand and an amulet on my belt in the other. Jerome brought his hands up.

"Joy!" I said when she emerged from the undergrowth, Naomi close behind her. "What are you doing here? Are you okay?"

"We just got away," she panted, her hand on her side as if she suffered from a stitch. "Those townsfolk are mean. One had a shovel, if you'd believe it."

"The amulets are working a treat, though." Naomi grinned. "Knocked three of them out, and the other two won't stop crying for the next ten minutes. Inconsolable. I love that amulet—totally non-violent, but always effective."

"We came across Denise, though," Joy said with a meaningful glance at me. "Definitely loyal to the order. If we hadn't had the elder amulets, we wouldn't be here."

"But you defeated her?" I said.

"Handily." Naomi amended her words when Joy glanced at her. "Maybe not handily, but we did it. And I got her amulets, too. They're not super powerful, so I amped them up a bit. And I had to crack the trigger word, no biggie, so now we have more." She tossed one to me, and I caught it despite my surprise. "Say 'vexo' and your enemy won't be able to stand, they'll be so shaky. Here's one for you, too, big guy."

She gave one to Jerome, who took it as carefully as one would handle a newborn baby. Magic still didn't sit comfortably with him, although he was doing far better than I had any right to expect.

Caelus swooped closer to Jerome's new amulet.

"If you transfer Jerome's spent amulet threads to this new one, won't that increase its strength?" he asked Naomi.

"Yes!' Naomi jumped forward and mashed the two amulets together. She performed a complex movement of her fingers accompanied by closed eyes and a low hum. Her eyes popped open. "So much better. I love having you around, Caelus."

"See?" he said to me. "Someone appreciates me."

"I appreciate you, you needy elemental," I rolled my eyes. "Come on, we need to keep moving."

"What do we do?" Joy said, her normally rich voice high with strain. "Now that we're here?"

I gazed at her. Although I was sorely tempted to take the reins, I didn't. Joy was clever in her own right, and she would think of things from a different perspective from me. I wasn't the expert here.

"Trust yourself, Joy," I said finally. "What do you think would be best?"

Joy searched my face, but I didn't give her any hints.

"Circle around again," she said. "Now that Denise is down, hopefully the way will be clear. Naomi has an amulet that masks the sound of us walking through the woods when she remembers to use it. We'll sneak in as close as we can."

"Good," I said with approval. I dug into my pocket and took out the confidence-boosting amulet key that I'd stolen from the elders' cabin. Joy could use it right now. "Say 'magna' and you'll feel much better. Now, go."

Joy and Naomi activated their amulets, and the two jogged silently through the woods, back the way they came.

I glanced at Jerome. "Onward, my doughty companion."

"I have no idea what that means, but I'll take it as a compliment."

168

The forest was close and contained-feeling. Wind whistled through the branches high above us, but below was still and quiet. No birds sang, and the only sound was the wind and our quiet footsteps on the dirt path.

At the sound of a cracking twig, I gripped Jerome's hand. His fingers were warm and firm under my grasp.

Two familiar figures stepped out from behind a tree. I squeezed Jerome's hand and then released it to ready myself for battle.

"Thea and Filippa Diamanto," I greeted them. "My lucky day."

"We knew you'd be coming," Thea said. Her smooth hair was immaculate as always. Filippa glowered behind her, the expression marring her otherwise beautiful face. "Your people aren't as under your thumb as you'd like to believe."

"Nobody is under anyone's thumb." I glanced at Jerome, and he nodded back, something metal clutched in his broad fist. Jerome was ready, and so was I. "We're a team. Sometimes a lack of control can backfire, but mostly, it produces brilliance. Not that you would understand. How is school these days now that you can't compel all your students into placid contentment?"

Thea curled her lip at me. "You think you're so clever, but you haven't met the full might of the order."

"Well, I escaped Hazel twice, so if you have more to show me, now is the time."

I pulled air threads toward me. Caelus glanced at the nearby lake.

"Think bigger, Morgan," he said. "The power of the air over a wide expanse of lake is immense. Pull on that."

My eyes flickered to the flat gray of the lake, but that instant of distraction was all it took for Thea to activate her amulet. With a shrieking trigger word, she released a flare of multicolored threads that enveloped me from head to toe.

CHAPTER XXI

I screamed as pain lanced through my body from Thea's amulet attack. My heartrate accelerated far past what was humanly possible. Would it burst out of my chest? I couldn't get nearly enough breath in my restricted, agonized lungs.

Jerome's warm hand gripped my shoulder. With his other hand, he pressed his protection amulet against the skin of my neck.

Instantly, my heartrate lowered, and I could breathe again, but Filippa didn't let her opportunity pass by. With her own amulet, she made a motion that mimed throwing something.

The ball of threads bounced harmlessly off our protection barrier, but it took a layer of strands with it. I stared in dismay at the thinning barrier.

"It won't hold forever," Caelus yelled. "Use the lake, now!"

"Distract them," I said to Jerome. I grabbed every air thread I could reach and yanked sideways. Every fiber of my essence thrummed with my intention to pull the vast mass of turbulent air off the lake and in a shooting jet toward Thea and Filippa.

Jerome blasted shot after shot of threads at the other two. One hit Thea, and her body shuddered uncontrollably as if in the throes of a seizure. Filippa was so busy ducking that she didn't have time to react to the tremendous roar that approached.

A blast of hurricane-force air slammed into the two and bowled them over, legs flying in grotesque cartwheels. Thea smacked into a tree and plastered against it, unmoving, while Filippa landed in a frantically swaying cluster of prickly Oregon grape bushes.

The wind hit me, too, but not nearly with the same force as the others. Jerome and I bent our knees and leaned into the gust until it passed. When it faded, branches still raining down in the forest, the silence was overwhelming.

"Thea's down," I whispered to Jerome. "I don't know where Filippa is. Let's get out of here."

I froze at the sound of crashing, and I gripped Jerome's arm to stop him. Filippa rose from the bushes, her hair wild and her eyes wilder. She pointed a trembling hand at us, a bracelet clasped between her fingers. Her gaze landed on her unmoving mother, and her cheeks grew pale.

"What did you do?" Filippa screeched. She dropped the bracelet she held and threw herself at the motionless Thea.

I pulled Jerome, and he followed, unresisting. This was our chance to escape and get closer to the spring head. We didn't get far before a weak cry stopped us. We found Shu and Lin huddled behind a boulder dripping with ferns. Lin was pale and clutched a hand to her side.

Shu looked at me with panic, her face lacerated with hundreds of tiny cuts that released a steady stream of blood to the forest floor.

"Morgan," she gasped. "Help her, please."

Time was ticking, but I couldn't leave Lin in this state. She was a member of the team—if I'd had any doubts about the former mother, they'd been vanquished at the sight of her injury—and she deserved to be healed.

"I'll do the best I can for now." I kneeled at Lin's side and reached for the knots in her threads. "Stop the bleeding, mainly. I'll fix her up better once we've stopped Hazel."

"I'll go get her," Shu said, standing. "Filippa destroyed my amulets, but we can still sneak up on Hazel. Come on, Jerome."

"Shu." Lin put out her hand, pleading. "Please, no. Stay with me. Hazel is too dangerous."

Shu stared at her mother, her face twisted with indecision. I massaged out Lin's largest knot and stood.

"She should be fine for now," I said. "I need to get to Hazel."

"I can clear your way," Shu said with determination. "Get

rid of the other order members."

"Me too," Jerome said. "No one will disturb you while you get the Thorn. You need to go straight there without any other distractions. We've got this."

Lin struggled to her feet. She was ghastly pale and wobbled unsteadily, but her face was set in a determined expression. "I can find Joy and Naomi and direct them to do the same."

I was pleased they'd decided that I was the best person to deal with Hazel—a fact I fully agreed with—but relying on Shu, Jerome, and Lin to keep everyone else away was difficult to accept.

But I had to. We were a team, and I had to trust that they would do their job without my guidance and oversight. I had no idea how they would get rid of the order, but I needed to let them figure it out while I focused on my task.

"Okay," I said finally. "But first, take these amulets, Shu." I unclipped two from my belt and handed them to her. "The green keychain makes your opponent move very slowly. Trigger word is 'gecko'. Say 'ibex' for the copper disc, and the area will turn pitch black for a minute. You'll have to figure out if it's useful on the fly. Use your judgment. I trust you."

Shu nodded solemnly. "Thanks, Morgan." She tucked the amulets in her pocket. "We won't let you down. And if you need backup, just shout. We'll figure something out, I promise."

I wasn't convinced of that, but I didn't think the situation would devolve that far. Hazel was only one woman, even if she were practically immortal and fluent in amulet-casting.

"Okay," I said. "Clear the way to the spring head. Hazel is due for a reckoning."

Lin stumbled through the woods toward where we thought Joy and Naomi might be now. Shu took a wide circling path toward the spring head, and Jerome followed me.

"Might as well clear your path right in front of you," he murmured, and I squeezed his hand.

The breeze in the treetops above lent a haunting drone to the silence in the forest. I expected to be ambushed at any moment by order members, and my grip on Jerome's hand tightened with every heartbeat.

Murmured voices carried on the breeze. We both stopped, then I dragged Jerome into the trees on the left.

"Are they coming our way?" I hissed.

Jerome peeked around the mossy trunk. "No. Let's sneak up and take a look."

I held my breath as we tiptoed away from our tree and along the edge of the path. The voices grew louder but were still indistinct.

"There are five of them." Caelus' words were deafening in the quiet forest.

I jumped and pressed a hand to my overactive heart. My glare would have scorched earth and leveled cities, but Caelus was unrepentant as always. He scanned the forest before us. I didn't dare reply to him in case our opponents heard.

Jerome waved me forward with an urgent hand. I peeked through the bush he crouched behind.

Four women encircled a girl on the ground. I recognized the girl as Sarah, the youngest member of the sisterhood. Her round cheeks were pale and her brown eyes wide, and my heart squeezed.

"Why are you doing this?" she cried. "I don't want to be here anymore. This is all wrong. I just want to go home."

Miranda stood with a glassy stare toward the lake, and Jasmine looked queasy beside her. Wanda pressed her boot against Sarah's chest, pinning the girl down. Amanda crossed her arms, her lips pursed.

Anger flooded my system at the sight of Amanda. "You," I snarled. I removed my hand from Jerome's and leaped forward.

"Get the betrayer," Caelus hissed.

"Morgan." Amanda uncrossed her arms, and Jasmine held up an amulet at the ready. Sarah's tear-streaked face stared at me, and Amanda tossed her head. "It was almost too easy to trick you. I'm quite proud of my acting skills. Maybe I'll audition for the movies after this is over."

"How long were you against us?" I asked, needing to know the answer but not wanting it.

"Right from the beginning," she replied, hands on hips. Miranda shuffled beside Amanda, her face placid. "And you never guessed. I knew as soon as I heard your plans that the order needed to know what was happening behind the scenes. So many members who lost faith! It's astonishing, really." She poked Sarah's leg with her foot. "Even Sarah here is having doubts."

"I don't think it's astonishing." I tilted my head. "Have you never questioned your order's laws? The truth of the Book of Souls? Why the mothers and elders hide secrets from the sisters? The power imbalance?"

"It makes sense," Amanda said without a flicker of doubt. "We have to prove ourselves in the trenches before we are worthy of the greater mysteries. Every mother and elder went through the same process and earned their rights. The sisters who don't agree clearly aren't worthy to ascend."

I waved at Miranda. "And how do you justify taking over your sister's mind and making her do your will?"

"She should have kept faith," Amanda replied with assurance. "I'm helping her keep her vows. She'll thank me later."

I couldn't reason with a fanatic. One of my hands inched to my amulet belt while the other twisted air threads in preparation.

"Get ready," I whispered to Jerome through immobile lips. He shifted his feet and slowly brought his hands to his pockets.

"Be careful with Miranda, she's under control. We need to save Sarah, too. I don't care about Amanda and the others."

He nodded slightly, his eyes never leaving the five young women before us.

I took a step. "Now that you've finally shown me your true colors, I know where I stand with you." I stepped forward again, and Amanda tensed. "But I have to get to the Thorn, and you're in my way."

Amanda grinned, and the mockery of her usual open smile tore a hole in my chest. How had she been so duplicitous? I'd thought we were friends. I'd trusted her as part of the team. How could I have been so blind?

"You'll have to get through us first," she said and plunged her hand into her pocket. Jerome dived sideways to engage Jasmine.

"Throw it!" Caelus yelled.

I threw my air ball at Amanda before she could counter. It flew and hit her in the stomach. She bent over, wheezing for lack of air in her lungs, but she wasn't down. With a flick and a whispered trigger word, rainbow threads shot from her hand and latched onto my shoulder.

The pain was excruciating. Thousands of tiny cuts pierced the exposed skin of my neck and cheek, digging in like shards of glass and twisting for extra agony. I grunted and grabbed an amulet. I could hardly see for tears streaming down my face, but I said the trigger word despite the searing pain.

Amanda stiffened and leaped around as if walking on hot coals and covered her eyes and ears with her arms. The amulet I'd triggered heightened her senses well past the point of comfort. By the looks of it, the world was too bright, too loud, and her feet too sensitive to touch. It would keep her busy for a moment while I dealt with my own issues.

"Pull the threads away," Caelus instructed. "Quickly, now. With intention."

I grimaced at Caelus' obvious commands but didn't waste

time bantering with him. My fingers grasped the rainbow threads at my neck and yanked.

Sweet relief crawled over my skin with the cessation of pain. I panted, but a grunt turned my head. Jasmine and Jerome were exchanging blows. Jerome's protection amulet was still activated—its strands wrapped around his body in a threadbare but comprehensive pattern—but Jasmine was no slouch. She'd clearly used an amulet on herself to bestow extra strength, and now she channeled that power into attacking Jerome physically. He was a match for her, but only just.

Wanda continued to hold Sarah down, but her expression clearly telegraphed her desire to join her sisters in battle. She thrust a hand into her pockets to do damage from afar.

"Nice try," I whispered. My fingers yanked at air threads, then I let an air ball fly. It hit Wanda directly on her chest.

She backed away, then her movements grew slower and slower. Her lips changed to a fleshy blue, and her eyelashes were rimmed with ice. Sarah scrambled away and fled into the trees. I hoped she would find a safer part of the forest.

Miranda still stared vacantly at the lake. Amanda must not have activated her control before attacking me, for which I was grateful. My attention zeroed in on the last opponent standing.

Jasmine landed a blow on Jerome's jaw, and it snapped his head around. My chest expanded with hot fury, but I didn't know how to separate the two without causing harm to both.

"Whip up the lake," Caelus shouted at me. "Get a wave to wash over them. That'll distract them."

I nodded. Amanda was still dealing with her sensitivities and would be for the next minute. I had time to save Jerome.

I gathered air threads and lifted my body to the lake. My feet skimmed over the water's choppy surface.

"Now what?" I yelled at Caelus.

"Whip it up," he shouted back. "Fly around in circles, lots of intention. Then fly back to Jasmine."

Caelus' instructions were terribly unspecific as usual, but

I'd played with air powers for long enough to know that intention was eighty percent of the battle. I flew in tight circles, concentrating hard on pulling air and dragging the water underneath. It frothed and rose in high waves that sloshed against my boots.

"To the shore," Caelus roared.

I switched direction and beelined to the trees. A whoosh of water followed me. I doubled down on my intention, and the wave of water turned into a wall.

"Hold your breath, Jerome," I screamed. He looked up, his eyes growing wide, and dived aside. Jasmine glanced up at my shout. She didn't have time to react before my water swept over her and knocked her down, along with the frozen Wanda.

It drenched Jerome and Miranda, too, but I concentrated hard on reducing the force on them, and they were merely wet, not knocked over. Amanda was still writhing around in the far trees and missed the deluge. I released my hold on the wave, and water sloshed to the ground and flowed back to the lake. Jasmine sputtered as I drifted next to her.

"I'm sorry, Jasmine," I said quietly. "But you picked the wrong side."

I reached out to tie together her strands so she couldn't move, but her hand darted out. A searing pain that burned like fire jabbed into my calf. I shrieked my agony and surprise to the forest canopy.

Jasmine gazed up at me with hard eyes, her hand clutched around an amulet. I bared my teeth at her.

"Suddenly, I'm not so sorry." I yanked at her strands, and she fell onto her face. With swift moves, trying to ignore the throbbing in my leg, I twisted her arm threads behind her back. The restraints would hold for at least half an hour. If that wasn't enough, then no doubt Jasmine would be the least of my worries.

I glanced at Miranda, still standing motionless, although she was soaked from her head to her running shoes. No gold chain winked at me from under the lank strands of her hair, and my heart sank. Hazel must have the Leaf and Seed.

"Morgan," Jerome gasped. He clutched his side, and his pale face registered alarm. He fumbled for an amulet, but his hands were slick with blood. "Amanda's coming."

Jerome was badly hurt, and I needed to tend to him, but Amanda's approach didn't let me. Anger coursed through my veins. Amanda had betrayed us. It was time she got what she deserved.

Her usually open face was twisted in rage. She stalked through the forest undergrowth toward me, branches slashing her face unheeded. "You're not getting the Thorn," she cried. "Not if I have anything to say about it."

Amanda slashed at the air with an amulet in each hand. Two jets of threads flew toward me, and I didn't have time to duck either of them.

My limbs grew weak, almost too weak to hold my body upright. At the same time, a wave of exhaustion flowed over me. I could have sunk to the ground and slept forever. I didn't have the energy to worry about Amanda's approach as she strode my way.

"Morgan," Caelus hissed at me. "Fight it off. It's an amulet."

"I can't," I moaned. "I'm too tired. My muscles are hardly working."

"You don't need to move much to use air powers," he insisted. "That tree needs a prune. Send it Amanda's way."

My eyes rolled slowly to the tree Caelus pointed at. It was clearly dead, its bark gray and withered. I twitched my fingers to gather silver threads. Amanda grinned and stopped with her arms crossed a few paces away from me.

"You think you're so clever," she said. "But you don't know the power of a well-oiled machine like the order. With Hazel in the driver's seat, we'll bring utopia to Earth, even with your meddling."

I forced my intention through the few threads I'd gathered and pulled. I hoped it was enough because it was all I had.

A deep groan shook my core. Amanda looked up, startled, but little was faster than a falling tree. It crashed down beside her, the trunk narrowly missing her body. The same couldn't be said for its branches. Amanda crumpled when a branch swiped her head and pinned her against the ground.

Amanda's distraction released my body from its own confines. I leaped to Jerome's side. His breaths were short and quick, and his mouth was tight with pain.

"Hold on," I muttered. My own injuries throbbed and stung, but Jerome needed my help immediately. If he bled out—I couldn't let myself think about it.

He held still while I massaged knots out of the threads above his wound. Miranda dropped to her knees beside me.

"I tied up Wanda and Amanda," she said quietly. "Wanda was almost thawed. Amanda's control on me broke when she was knocked out."

"Thanks." I spared her a brief smile. "It's good to have you back."

Miranda's face twisted. "I can't believe Amanda."

"Best not to dwell." My fingers unpicked Jerome's knots with all the swiftness I could muster. "Focus on the battle before us. We still need to get to the Thorn."

Slowly, Jerome's bleeding stopped, and his face relaxed from its rictus of pain.

"Thanks," he said. He pushed my hands aside and struggled to his feet. I held onto his arm for support. "But that's probably enough. We should get moving."

"Not so fast." Beatrice's voice carried in the quiet forest.

CHAPTER XXII

I whipped my head around so fast that my neck made a crunching noise. Jerome was probably losing feeling in his arm with the way I was squeezing it. Beatrice gazed at us, every one of her fingers adorned with a ring.

"That's a lot of amulets," Caelus muttered. "Watch out."

"Split up," I said to Jerome and Miranda and threw myself forward and sideways. I felt rather than saw Jerome and Miranda stumble to the other side and run in zigzag patterns into the forest.

Beatrice ignored Jerome. Instead, she pointed her left hand at me.

"You really are as much of a bother as Hazel claims." She trained her hand on me as I ran along the rocky edge of the lake. My foot slipped, and my boot crashed into the water. My next footstep landed with an unpleasant squelch. "And your elemental is clearly still with you. Luckily, I have what it takes to rid you of the pesky spirit. You won't get between me and my immortality."

I threw myself forward desperately, but Beatrice pointed and muttered an unintelligible word.

Deep, uncontrollable pain hit me right in the stomach. I screamed and dropped to my knees, but my scream wasn't the only sound. Caelus yelled in anguish, too. Gradually, through the agony, I realized that the sensation came from his threads. Whatever Beatrice was doing, it was ripping Caelus away from me. We were too entwined to forcibly part without consequence.

"Don't let go," I gasped. "Caelus, stay with me." The lancing jabs pierced me with fiery torment.

Caelus' face was contorted. "I'm trying," he wheezed. Then his eyes fluttered closed, and his body dissolved into his component threads.

"No!" I screamed. A loud thud echoed through the woods, and the pain miraculously stopped. I kneeled over my knees, panting, then I glanced to the side. Jerome stood over Beatrice's motionless body, a thick branch in his hands. Miranda held an amulet in front of her, presumably used as a distraction while Jerome snuck up from behind.

Beatrice wasn't a worry anymore, so I focused on Caelus. I scooped up the loose cluster of silver threads that floated in midair before me. "Hold on, Caelus," I muttered. "This isn't done. We're not over yet."

When his threads were safely gathered at my stomach, I carefully plucked a few of my strands and wrapped them over Caelus to hold him against me. I had no idea what Beatrice had done to Caelus, whether he would recover, or if my actions would do any good, but I had to do something.

When his threads were secure against mine, I stood and took shaky steps toward Jerome. My entire body felt bruised, my elbow was throbbing even through my previous pain remedy, my neck stung like fire, and a trickle of blood ran from my nose. I wiped it away with my sleeve, too battered to worry about hygiene.

"Are you okay?" Jerome carefully wrapped me in his arms, and I leaned against him for a moment of respite. Sometimes it was hard being the competent one. Sharing the load wasn't as bad as I'd always imagined. Jerome pushed me away and looked at my face. "Talk to me."

"I'm okay," I said. "But Caelus is hurt. I don't know what happened to him. He's still there, but I can't reach him."

"Do you still have your powers?" Miranda asked, her brow contracted.

I gathered a few threads of air and pushed them at Jerome's face. He blinked at the sudden light breeze.

"I guess so," I said. "So, there's still hope for Caelus."

"And for the Thorn," he said.

"The Thorn." In the tumult and my shock of losing Caelus,

I'd almost forgotten our mission. What would the joining of the artifacts be like? Would we know when the destruction started? "We need to move."

A small cabin, little more than a utility shed, lay directly ahead on the water's edge. I knew—from a previous visit to Harrison many years ago—that the spring head burbled up inside the shed, and pipes took hot water to the town. Water leaked from the door of the shed and ran toward the lake, steaming in the cool morning air. Now that I was finally here, I wondered where the Thorn would be in that mess of plumbing. I wished I'd had the luxury of time to look. Maybe Hazel had already found it. The thought didn't comfort me.

"There it is," Jerome whispered. "I guess Hazel's already inside."

"I'll find the others," Miranda breathed. "We need backup." She trotted into the woods and disappeared.

Without warning, Jerome tugged me around to face him. His piercing eyes drove into me. Then, he swooped down and kissed my mouth hard.

I opened my mouth for him, the adrenaline of the morning pulsing through my veins and heightening the sensation of his desperate kiss. His tongue slid inside, and I groaned. Quietly, since Hazel was too close for comfort.

Hazel. Reluctantly, I pushed Jerome's chest. Our lips parted, and he sighed.

"Be careful, okay?" He gave me a stern look. "I'll be looking for more of that once this is all done."

I chuckled breathlessly. "It's a date."

A crack of someone stepping on a branch sounded in the near distance. Jerome stiffened, then he leaped forward on near-silent footfalls to hunt down whoever had made the noise. I shivered. I wouldn't want to be on the wrong side of Jerome, no matter how many amulets I had. The right side, however…

I shook my head and crept forward, careful not to make a sound. When I grew closer, chanting in an unfamiliar language reached my ears.

I paused. What was my plan? Dueling in the tiny shed held little appeal, but drawing Hazel out would lose me the element of surprise. I glanced down at my belt, an idea forming in my mind. A plain disc of silver on my belt winked at me. With a touch and a word, it would disintegrate whatever it touched. At the time Naomi had explained it, I'd recoiled in disgust. I didn't want to disintegrate anyone, no matter how they'd wronged me. It sounded like a horrible way to die.

But what if I reduced the building to ash? A smile crept onto my face, and I tiptoed closer. I unclasped the keychain from my belt and held it to the surface of the shed. Hazel's chanting grew louder. I opened my mouth, took a deep breath, and whispered the trigger word.

"Blubber."

A sound like shifting sand reached my ears. The shed wall shimmered, grew indistinct, then turned into a million grains of sand and collapsed to the forest floor.

Hazel stood with her back to me and her arms raised, but she spun around with a look of shock when the shed disappeared. She must have used a similar amulet on the pipes because there were none. Instead, her rubber boots stood ankle deep in hot water that gushed from a gap in the stone behind her. Candles burned on the top of sturdy metal holders stuck into the ground with water flowing around them. Brown threads from the earth swirled around blue water strands, which joined silver air threads and orange ones from the hot spring's heat. All the elements were represented at this place.

Hazel wore a long tan-colored robe embroidered at the edges of the long sleeves with a strange alphabet that looked suspiciously like cuneiform. I wondered suddenly exactly how old Hazel was. She was clearly performing a ceremony to get the Thorn, not simply planning to mash the artifacts together. That worked for me, because if she had been more impatient, then I would have been too late to stop her.

As soon as the building collapsed, I pulled a gust of wind toward Hazel and readied another amulet. The wind blew out the candles and knocked one holder over. Hazel clutched at her robe in the strong gust.

I said the trigger word for my amulet. Nothing happened except for a glow of threads around Hazel. She must have been holding a protection amulet.

Hazel smiled and slashed an amulet at me. Time sped up, or was I simply slower? I watched in horrified fascination as Hazel held out an amulet and said a word in Latin. I was powerless to stop her.

A crunch of bone snapping broke me out of my trance. I screamed and stumbled sideways. My thigh was twisted at an odd angle, and I nearly threw up from pain and disgust.

I fell on my bottom on the muddy ground next to the hot water flow, winded and consumed with agony. Hazel stepped toward me. With a satisfied smile, she held up the artifact locket from a pocket in her robe.

"Thank you for delivering the Leaf and Seed to Harrison."

I closed my eyes briefly, overwhelmed by my failure. Not only was I injured and at Hazel's mercy, but I had unwittingly brought exactly what she needed to the Thorn's resting place. Why hadn't I left the locket in the city? I didn't have a safe place for the artifacts, but surely anywhere was better than here.

"Why didn't you steal back the artifacts earlier? You knew where we were. Amanda must have told you everything."

"You had them safe." Hazel frowned her displeasure. "Your wards were better than you realized. No one could get into your safe houses without an invitation, and I didn't trust Amanda to do my bidding with the finesse I required. I knew an opportunity would present itself eventually. If there's one thing I have in abundance, it's patience."

"What's the point of having people on your side if you can't trust them?"

Hazel gazed at me. "My people managed to strip away all of your so-called followers. The order might not be good for much, but they do know how to follow instructions." She chuckled darkly. "Especially when coerced by magic. You should have followed my example and taken tighter control of your group. Who knows, maybe you would have prevailed. Unlikely, but you would have had a better chance."

"They aren't my followers," I ground out. "They're my team." Despite the pain I was in, and my vulnerability before Hazel, I felt a surge of pride. Together, we had brought me this far. I'd relied on my team, trusted them to do what they thought was best, and they had supported me. I might not win here, but we'd given it our best shot. Together, as equals. "You wouldn't understand that. You've always worked alone."

"Not for long." Hazel plunged her hand into the spring and rummaged around. Her skin reddened and blistered, but she ignored the pain she must be in from the hot water. "I'll join the artifacts now, then Spirit will return, and we will be together forever. I've waited since my youth thousands of years ago, cradled between the Tigris and the Euphrates."

Inwardly, I marveled at Hazel's immense age—was she an ancient Sumerian or Babylonian?—and quailed that I was pitting myself against someone with millennia of experience. How did I expect to win against her?

"What about Beatrice and Agatha's immortality?" I didn't care about them—no one should be immortal, least of all members of the order—but I had to keep Hazel talking. I inched forward, wincing with every pull along the ground I performed. I felt like a caterpillar. A bleeding, mangled, broken caterpillar.

Hazel scoffed, her hand still in the water. "Agatha and Beatrice were a means to an end. Releasing Spirit is my goal.

I don't care who drops their blood on the Seed at the crucial moment."

Hazel drew out a small lead box the size of her palm with her raw and reddened hand. I was finally close enough to push to my good leg with shaking arms. I held out my switchblade, ready to cut Hazel wherever it hurt.

Hazel laughed, a deep, throaty cackle that sent shudders down my spine.

"You can't kill me," she said. "Or, if you do, I'll just come back. As long as my ring artifact is intact, I will remain on earth to complete my mission. Spirit is relying on me."

She held up her hand with an expression of triumph. The ring on her left hand glowed with threads next to the locket in her palm. Everything on me hurt, and I could barely focus on Hazel because of my broken femur. Hazel held the Leaf and Seed in one hand, and the Thorn in a box with the other. She watched me with intense eyes and a small smile as she clicked open the rotating clasp that held the box closed.

I could lunge forward with my knife, but Hazel's hand also held the amulet that had broken my leg. I knew it could do the same to any other limb of my body. I had nothing left, no way to defeat Hazel. I could only watch her join the artifacts together and bring Spirit to Earth.

But I wasn't alone. There was one last thing I could do.

"Shu!" I screamed into the forest. "Jerome! Anyone!"

Silence reigned. Hazel laughed, cold and cruel.

"I told you, you should have controlled your followers better." She tsked and grabbed the Thorn with her hand that held the other two artifacts. With triumph, she raised the three together in the air.

The sun disappeared. All light faded from the world in a heartbeat. When it left, darkness reigned. And not the darkness of a city night when streetlights glowed through curtains and eyes could adjust to the dim. Shu had activated her amulet at my call. This dark was absolute.

Except for my eyes. The threads of the world glowed softly and outlined objects before me. Silver threads drifted in the air and the spring burbled with blue and orange strands. Hazel's form was clearly delineated in purple and green threads, and the artifacts shimmered with rainbow colors.

I leaped forward with my last strength. My blade slashed down. With a hot spray of blood that landed on my exposed skin, the blade sliced through Hazel's wrist like warm butter. Her hand flew away with the force of my blow and landed with a thump on the forest floor, away from the river of hot water. The artifacts landed in a circle around it.

Hazel screamed and clutched her bleeding stump to her chest. I didn't waste time attending to her. Instead, I scrambled toward her severed hand, trying not to gag at the sight now that the darkness was already lifting from my eyes, and grabbed my silver disc amulet. I pressed the disc against her immortality ring.

The hand and its ring shimmered and dissolved into a million fragments with a hushed sound like running sand. I could barely hear it over Hazel's shrieks. Nothing was left of the artifact.

Hazel's yells changed timbre, and I turned to stare at her. She twitched and moaned, her movements unnaturally jolting, like a dying insect. Her eyes rolled up into her face. Then, with puffs of green and purple threads that drifted away in the breeze, Hazel's body dropped into the hot spring water, dead.

She was gone, and she hadn't joined the artifacts together. A brief pang of sympathy for Hazel ran through me—she would never join her lover in endless connection—but it was overwhelmed by relief that this was over. Now, I could destroy the artifacts just like Caelus wanted.

Was that what Caelus still wanted? After his meeting with Air, he'd had plenty of questions about his mission.

I shook my head. The artifacts were dangerous. I couldn't risk another order member joining them and striving for endless powers or immortality.

But I owed it to Caelus to get his opinion. We were a team, and I couldn't make this decision without his input. But how could I revive my poor elemental friend?

My eye fell on the locket, which had spilled open from the force of its fall. I grabbed the Seed, easy to spot on the ground, as it was covered in multicolored threads. With a burst of intention, I brought the Seed to the silver cluster where Caelus resided. I could heal everyone else's wounds with thread-vision, but I had no clue how to help Caelus. The Seed was my only idea.

"Here I go, Caelus," I muttered, then reached with intention for my heart. I thought about the banter Caelus and I shared, and how lost and alone I felt when he left me for Beaky.

Multicolored strands burst from the Seed and wrapped around me. My body seized, but I didn't allow the inevitable pain to distract me from my goal. I bent my will toward directing the Seed's healing power toward the sad cluster of silver threads at my stomach.

The colorful strands surrounded Caelus and pulsed to the beat of agony that my injuries throbbed with. For an eternity, the pain drove through every particle of me. Then, as suddenly as they'd arrived, the strands retreated and left me panting but pain-free.

Caelus burst out of my arm. "I'm back," he announced, then he looked around. "Did you get it?"

"We did."

I smiled around at the others, who had limped into view while I'd healed Caelus. Lin leaned against Shu, but she was upright and not as pale as before. Joy cradled her arm, supported by Miranda, and Naomi shuffled slowly, but their knots were simple to untangle. Jerome's side was still in need of attention, but I was happy to give him all my attention when we got back to Vancouver.

"Now," I said to Caelus. "Are you ready to destroy the

artifacts?"

Caelus nodded solemnly. "It needs to be done, no matter what I think of Air. The Book of Souls contained too many hints of Earth's destruction to ignore, which is always bad for the balance. It's time."

I moved the Leaf to the ground in front of me, then I placed the Seed on top.

"That disintegration amulet should work," I said. "Let's put the artifacts together and use that."

I reached out and grasped the Thorn. It was a deep ebony black with an elegant curve ending in a wicked point.

Somehow, my fingers fumbled. The tip of the Thorn pierced my fingertip.

"Ow!" I snatched my hand back, but the gash the Thorn left in my finger was deep and wide. Droplets of blood sprinkled the ground in front of me. One landed directly on the Seed.

"Uh oh," Caelus whispered.

CHAPTER XXIII

Threads shot out from the Seed, grabbing, pulling, grasping at other threads nearby. I scrabbled backward, my heart in my throat.

"What do I do?" I yelled at Caelus. "My blood must have got on it."

"I don't know!" He sounded as panicked as I felt. He waved at the writhing mass of threads. "Kick it or something."

"What's happening?" Shu shouted. "Why is the Seed glowing? Did you activate it?"

I crawled toward the Seed, determined to wrestle it into submission, but threads lashed out at me. They held me at bay, so however hard I strained to get closer, I never closed the distance.

"I can't get to it," I panted. "How do I stop this?"

Flapping made my head twist upward. Wings crossed between me and the sky in an ominous shadow, but it was only Beaky. Had she followed me here?

The pigeon landed with a flutter and folded her wings in. She cooed once then strutted forward, directly into the wriggling mass of strands. With her beak, she stabbed at the Seed and Leaf and held both in her mouth. Threads dribbled from her head like colorful spaghetti.

Without warning, she opened her wings and flapped into the air. Within seconds, she was far above the trees.

"Jump to her," I yelled at Caelus. "Make her come back!"

"She's too far away," he said in a tone of disbelief. "I can't reach her. How could we be so close to destroying the artifacts and yet utterly miss our target?"

I glanced at the Thorn, the only part of the equation still resting on the ground. Its job was complete, and as I watched, it slowly disintegrated into dust and blew away in a breeze from the lake.

"Now what?" Joy said faintly, leaning on Naomi for support. "The Seed is germinated. Exactly what we were trying to stop."

I pushed to my feet and dusted off my knees. It was a futile effort. Every piece of clothing was dirty, battered, and torn. I wanted to wail with frustration, but that wasn't what we needed now.

"We stopped Hazel," I said firmly. "She was ruthless and used the order for her own gain. We also stopped the rest of the order from accessing the artifacts. We have plenty to celebrate." I took a deep breath. "Yes, the Seed is germinated. The Tree of Life is growing as we speak. But trees grow slowly." I hoped that was the case here. It was likely that the Tree was a magical one and lived by its own schedule, but I didn't want to worry the team with negativity like that. "And we have plenty of time to find it and destroy it so that this Spirit elemental doesn't begin her reign of terror."

"Wait," Lin said. She narrowed her eyes at me. "Your blood started the Tree. Does that mean you've gained immortality?"

My eyes widened, and I stared at my bloody fingertip. Is that what had happened? If the Book of Souls was to be believed, I now possessed the ability to live forever. Was I invincible, or simply long-lasting? My double lifetime was fun, but I couldn't imagine doing it forever.

"I don't know," I said eventually. "I guess we'll find out. I hope not. Eternity is a long time."

I healed our subdued group. Once everyone was feeling better physically, our disappointment with the Tree gave way to jubilation over defeating Hazel. No one seemed particularly fussed that she'd died.

"She's been living for millennia," Shu said. "She had her fair share of life."

We walked back along the path together. Shu and Naomi stopped at an unconscious Beatrice and hauled her along with us. Amanda, Jasmine, and Wanda were no longer at the fallen tree—one must have recovered enough to help the others—and I was happy to avoid seeing them again. When we reached motionless Thea with a battered and angry-looking Filippa next to her, I stopped.

"I can heal your mother," I said. "If you'll let me."

"Why would you do that?" Filippa snapped.

"Because it's over, Filippa," Joy said loudly. "Hazel is dead, and the artifacts are gone. We won, and we don't want to see anyone else die today."

She carefully worded her message to avoid saying what had really happened to the artifacts. I'd forgotten to tell the others that they should keep quiet about the possibility that the Tree was growing in a remote location. I needn't have bothered worrying. It was clear that my team could be relied upon.

Filippa stared at us for a long time. Then, her shoulders slumped, and she collapsed against a tree trunk.

"Fine," she said, her words muffled by hands over her face. "Heal my mother, if you can."

I walked over and kneeled at Thea's side. The bruise on her head looked nasty, and her eyes were unresponsive when I peeled back her eyelids.

"Start with the head," Caelus said. "If she's going to make it, that will be the deciding factor."

While I unpicked knots, the others went out in groups and scoured the forest for other order members. Shu and Lin found some bewildered townsfolk and escorted them back to the forest's edge. The others brought order members who were hurt in battle and laid them out for me to help. Joy rummaged in everyone's pockets for amulets and collected them in a pile on the forest floor.

It took a solid fifteen minutes of untangling before Thea groaned and sat up. Filippa hugged her mother fiercely, and

Thea looked around blearily at us.

"What's going on?" she murmured.

"Filippa will fill you in on the details," I said shortly. "Suffice it to say, your order days are done." I tossed the silver disintegration disc to Naomi and pointed at the amulet pile. "If you'll do the honors?"

Naomi looked sadly at the pile, but she held the amulet against it and said the trigger word. Within a few seconds, the pile turned to dust and fell in a heap in the dirt.

Thea blinked furiously.

"So, that's it," she said softly. "All our hopes and dreams, our beliefs, our whole way of living. Gone in an instant."

"Time to put your faith in something more rewarding." I stood and stretched before moving to an unconscious Beatrice. "Maybe endless power isn't the best thing to strive for. Endless compassion, maybe. Or justice. Or equality. Or any one of a slew of virtues. Take your pick."

I healed the order members enough that they could limp to town. I wasn't feeling any more charitable than that. Each one of my team hugged me at the parking lot, and I took the opportunity to remind them not to mention the Tree to anyone.

I stuck to Jerome's side like a burr as my team got in their cars and drove away. He slipped his hand into mine.

"I take it you'd like a ride home?" he said quietly.

I squeezed his hand. "If you're heading my way, stranger."

His old truck had a bench seat, so I sat in the middle and he drove with my head on his shoulder. We didn't speak much, and it was exactly what I wanted. The last week had been a whirlwind of stress, hiding, searching, and kidnapping, culminating in today's battle. I wanted a little slice of calm.

"It's a long drive out to Harrison," Caelus said.

Jerome flinched, and I groaned. "I'm so glad you're okay,

Caelus. But could you please tuck into your cluster at my stomach for a while?"

"Humph." He didn't retreat to my stomach, but he was silent for a while. I returned my head to Jerome's shoulder.

"Open your window," Caelus said suddenly when we were at a traffic light. "Quickly."

I grumbled but obeyed. Flapping and cooing filled the opening, and I ducked. Beaky balanced on the window ledge. Quickly, I pushed Caelus' strands toward her. All the silver threads Beaky had brought in with the wind faded from view.

"Thanks, Caelus," I whispered. Beaky took off in an explosion of feathers and flapped in the direction of home.

"He's gone?" Jerome said gruffly.

I patted his thigh. "It's just you and me."

When we passed the street that led to my condo, Jerome glanced at me. I shook my head, and we continued to his apartment. I didn't want to be alone, and I didn't want to deal with whatever mess Hazel had left in my condo. Jerome seemed to understand, and I ran my fingers over the back of his neck.

He led me down the hall of his apartment building. Inside, dishes waited for washing, and clothes were piled on the floor of his bedroom.

"I wasn't expecting company," he muttered.

I laughed. "I wasn't expecting to be company. And look." I twirled around to show him my torn and battered clothing. "I'm not particularly presentable today."

"Why don't you take a shower," he suggested with a raised eyebrow at my attire. "I hate to tell you, but you're pretty dirty."

I stepped closer and ran my hand up his chest. "I'd like to explore what dirty really means," I whispered and was gratified to see color appear on Jerome's cheeks. I patted his chest and stepped away. "But shower first."

I stifled a grin at Jerome's frustrated face and sauntered to the bathroom. Footsteps walked back and forth while I washed, and when I was done, I found a clean towel and a large tee shirt tucked inside the bathroom doorway.

I held up the shirt and shrugged. It was clean, and that was all I wanted right now. Well, that and a certain someone.

Jerome had tidied while I washed. Baking magazines were stacked neatly on the coffee table, the bed was made, and the smell of dish soap lingered in the air.

Jerome's jaw worked when he saw me in his tee shirt and nothing else, but I pointed at the bathroom.

"It's all yours."

When he emerged, hair wet and tousled in a deliciously pleasing way, I'd taken out the pizza from the oven that Jerome must have popped in from the freezer and was slicing it on the coffee table.

He sat, and I pointed at the pizza. "Hungry?"

"Yes." His eyes never left mine, and a pleasurable warmth crept over me. The pizza sat forgotten as Jerome leaned forward in sync with me. We met in the middle, and his hands covered my hips, my waist, my breasts. I pushed my hungry mouth against his and lay back on the couch, forcing him to follow me. His body pressed along mine with a solid, unyielding weight, and I wrapped my leg around his with pure desire.

CHAPTER XXIV

Jerome traced my shoulder with the tip of his finger as we lay curled on the couch after our long-awaited alone time.

"You're not afraid to tell me what you want, are you?" he murmured into my back.

I chuckled. "I've lived too long to close my eyes and think of England. If we're not both enjoying ourselves, what's the point?"

"I like it." He propped himself up on one arm, and I rolled to face him. His honey-colored eyes were warm with contentment. "Takes the guesswork out of everything. Feel free to order me around like that any day."

I sighed with happiness and satisfaction. My hands ran over the tattoos liberally inked on Jerome's chest and upper arms. I'd never considered tattoos to be a turn-on, but on Jerome they worked. They worked very well, in fact. Heat rose in my body, and I wondered if Jerome was ready for round two.

"They don't bother you?" he murmured when he noticed the direction of my gaze.

"Not at all."

"They only remind me of those years with my uncle. I'd like to get them all removed, but I can't afford that, and removal doesn't work as well as I'd like."

"You don't need to remove them." I rubbed my hand over his pectoral. Jerome flexed and I chuckled. "They're growing on me. Quite quickly, in fact."

Jerome's wicked smile grew slowly but surely. I continued my examination of his artwork. A gnarled tree caught my eye, and a niggling worry entered my mind to ruin the moment. I shifted, and my face must have announced my concern, for Jerome frowned.

"What's the matter?"

"The Tree of Life." I sighed again, but this time not so

happily. "After all that effort, the damn thing sprouted anyway. And now I have no idea where it is."

"It can't be far," Jerome said reasonably. "Beaky came back to the truck while we were driving here. We can hunt for it. Every day, if necessary, until we find it."

"You're right." I snuggled in closer to Jerome. It was nice to have people to rely on. And I truly felt that I could rely on Jerome, as well as my team. It was a novel sensation for me. "I don't know what we'll do when we find it."

"Chop it down? It is a tree, after all."

"We'll probably have to do something magical. Caelus might have an idea, or Naomi." I traced Jerome's jaw with my finger.

"We don't have to worry about the apocalypse happening tonight, do we?" Jerome stared at me.

I shook my head. "The Tree needs to mature before Spirit is released. We have some time."

"But it's a magic tree. How fast does it grow?"

Unease roiled in my gut. "I don't know. I'll start hunting for it tomorrow."

Jerome caressed my back, and I relaxed into the sensation. After a few minutes of gentle silence, he spoke again.

"It was your blood that germinated the Seed. So that means you're now immortal."

I shivered. Immortality was a loaded word. I wasn't exactly a stranger to time—I recalled my past lives, however vaguely—but to live this life with clarity for eternity felt daunting. And those I cared about would leave me sooner or later. A year ago, that might not have bothered me much. Now? My hand tightened on Jerome's waist.

"Maybe it's reversible," I said. "Immortality wasn't what I wanted. Maybe when we stop the Tree, the effects will fade."

"Maybe." Jerome kissed my forehead. "We'll figure it out. Together."

I tucked my head under Jerome's chin, happy to ignore an

uncertain future for the bliss of this moment.

"Together."

The window was still black when Jerome left for work. He kissed my forehead gently, but I wrapped my arms around him and gave him a sleepy embrace before he left.

"Call me later," I murmured.

"Always," he said.

When the sun woke me up for the second time, I rolled over and texted Joy. We needed a recap, and I needed coffee. I dressed in my jeans, unfortunately still torn and dirty from my exertions yesterday, and I wiped my leather jacket with a towel as best as I could to get the grime off. I swiped another tee shirt from Jerome's drawers—there was no way I was putting on mine from yesterday's battle—and left his apartment. I was looking forward to coming back later, though.

Beaky cooed from a tree on the boulevard, and the threads of the world blossomed in front of my eyes again.

"Welcome back," I said to Caelus. "Thanks for the privacy."

"Yeah, you owe me one," he grumbled. "Beaky is so chaotic in her head that my own mind wouldn't stop spinning. Luckily she slept for some of the night." He glanced at me slyly. "Your mating ritual must have been longer this time."

I couldn't help the broad grin that spread across my face. "Yes, it was."

Joy and Shu were waiting for me at Sacred Grounds when I arrived. Two young women I didn't recognize were serving behind the counter. I paid for my coffee and brought it to the table.

"Who are they?" I jerked my thumb at the two strangers where Amanda and Denise usually worked.

"On-call workers," Joy said. "Amanda and Denise both

phoned in sick, according to these two.”

“They don’t want to show their sorry faces in here, more like.” Shu rolled her eyes. “Sucks to pick the losing side.”

“I bet they’re at loose ends after Hazel’s death,” Joy said. “She really held everyone together. Beatrice isn’t the leader type, and Agatha might have had a heart attack after hearing about Hazel, who knows. Thea might pick up the slack, but I don’t know.”

“In any event,” I said. “I’m going to start hunting for the Tree today. My pigeon friend Beaky flew away with the germinated Seed, but she didn’t go far. If I have to hunt every square kilometer in her flying radius to find the Tree, then so be it. Preventing the apocalypse is too important.”

“Make sure you mark off where you’ve searched,” Joy said. “We can help after work and on our days off.”

I nodded then frowned. “Have you heard from Rosemary lately? I don’t know if she heard about the ruckus yesterday.”

“I saw her,” Joy said. “She wasn’t as manic as she has been. Maybe we destroyed whatever amulet was affecting her. She seemed calm, almost like she used to be. She didn’t take the news of the artifacts well—she was always hoping for utopia, even after everything—but she was sad, not crazy.”

I sighed. “I’m glad to hear it. She’s been on a rollercoaster. We all have.”

We sipped our respective drinks in silence, then Joy narrowed her eyes at me.

“You’re wearing the same thing you were yesterday, except for that extra-large shirt.” She grinned. “Do I detect a walk of shame?”

“No shame here.” I smiled at the memory of last night. “I was at Jerome’s. But I didn’t change before coming here because I couldn’t face my condo without coffee to fortify me. Hazel gave it a thorough trashing, according to Caelus. Holes in the walls and everything. I didn’t have the energy to face it this morning.”

Joy and Shu glanced at each other.

"Give us your key," Joy said with her hand out. "We'll fix it after work. Stay away until this evening."

"I redecorated our living room last year," Shu said proudly. "My girlfriend Jolene adores it. Your place is in good hands."

I wavered. Giving my key to these two would mean handing over all responsibility for my condo's décor. I would have no oversight over the details. Could I handle that? Did I trust them?

"Here." I dropped my key into Joy's outstretched hand. "Good luck. And thanks. Oh, take Naomi with you—there's an amulet waiting as a booby trap. She'll be able to disarm it."

Shu's gaze glanced at the door, and her eyes widened.

"Miranda." She half-stood, and I twisted in my seat, ready for anything.

Miranda approached our table with an apologetic expression. Her forehead was scrunched up, and she looked almost ready to burst into tears.

"I swear it wasn't my fault," she said when she was closer. "It was like I was watching my body do these terrible things and I couldn't do anything to stop it. I wasn't a mole, I swear."

"We know." I patted the seat next to me. "Join us."

Miranda slid into the seat but still looked ready to flee at the first sign of discontent. Joy reached across the table and grabbed her hand.

"We know Amanda was the only mole," she said in her warm voice. "She used an amulet on you when she visited the hotel yesterday morning."

"And a few other times," I said. "Miranda's despondency, Joy's slow-mindedness, Shu's excess energy, they were all the sort of subversive magic that characterizes elder amulets. Because I'd warded each of our secret locations, Hazel couldn't come herself, but she could send her emissary to infect us."

Miranda shivered. "I thought I would know who wasn't on

our side. Was Amanda controlled, too? Or was she just an amazing actor?"

"I don't know how to tell now that the amulets are destroyed," I said. "She could say anything, and we'd have no way to check. I think you have to resign yourself to the possibility that she might have been acting of her own free will."

The others sipped their drinks with gloomy expressions.

"I guess that's it for the order," Shu said finally. "End of an era."

"There's still the Tree to find," I reminded her. "Until the Tree is taken care of, the order's legacy remains a threat."

"We'll get it," Joy said firmly. "Together, we're unstoppable. Look what we managed yesterday!"

I grinned at her, buoyed by her enthusiasm. "We were quite the team."

I exited Sacred Grounds and took a deep breath of the crisp February air. A hint of the freshness of spring lingered in my lungs, and I rolled my shoulders back to draw in even more breath.

Caelus emerged from my arm. "Now what? Are we looking for the Tree today?"

"Today and every day until we find it." I strode toward the Skytrain terminal. "I'll rent a car, and we'll travel in circles around Harrison Hot Springs. How fast does a pigeon fly? I'll look at a map to see how far we have to search."

"We should be able to see the Tree clearly," said Caelus. "The threads alone will be a giveaway."

"What will we do when we find the Tree?"

Caelus looked discomposed. "Destroy it, I suppose. I wish we knew more about Spirit. The promised apocalypse was only written about in the Book of Souls. We have no other source."

"Except for historical records," I reminded him. "And overwhelming floods in multiple ancient mythologies."

Caelus huffed. "Still, what if this Spirit elemental is not as bad as she sounds?"

"What about your mission?" I reminded him. "Destroying artifacts for Air."

"But Air said artifacts were no big deal," Caelus said in a heated tone. "Air said to focus on the Leaf, Seed, and Thorn, and I still don't know why. Will chopping down the Tree of Life put me in Air's good graces? Will I be ruining something far greater by doing that? I have no answers."

I straightened my leather jacket and looked at Caelus with an intent eye.

"Then it's time to get some."

ALSO BY EMMA SHELFORD

Magical Morgan
Daughters of Dusk
Mothers of Mist
Elders of Ether

Immortal Merlin
Ignition
Winded
Floodgates
Buried
Possessed
Unleashed
Worshiped
Unraveled

Depths of Magic
Sea Fire

Nautilus Legends
Free Dive
Caught
Surfacing
Hooked

Forest Fae
Mark of the Breenan
Garden of Last Hope
Realm of the Forgotten

ACKNOWLEDGEMENTS

A hearty thanks to my readers Anna McCluskey, Bettina, and Nadene, for helping me polish Elders. Thanks to Deranged Doctor Design for pulling off another exciting cover.

ABOUT THE AUTHOR

Emma Shelford feels that life is only complete with healthy doses of magic, history, and science. Since these aren't often found in the same place, she creates her own worlds where they happily coexist. If you catch her in person, she will eagerly discuss Lord of the Rings ad nauseam, why the ancient Sumerians are so cool, and the important role of phytoplankton in the ocean.

Emma is the author of multiple urban fantasy series, including Magical Morgan, Immortal Merlin, Depths of Magic, Nautilus Legends, and Forest Fae.